T + R

D0553750

salt
water

Also by Charles Simmons

Powdered Eggs

An Old-Fashioned Darling

Wrinkles

The Belles Lettres Papers

salt water

a novel

CHARLES SIMMONS

CHRONICLE BOOKS
SAN FRANCISCO

Text copyright © 1998 by Charles Simmons.

All rights reserved. No part of this book may be reproduced in any form without written permission

from the publisher.

Library of Congress Cataloging-in-Publication Data available.

ISBN 0-8118-2182-X

Printed in the United States of America.

Designed by Carole Goodman

Composition by Neal Elkin

Distributed in Canada by Raincoast Books

8680 Cambie Street

Vancouver, British Columbia V6P 6M9

10 9 8 7 6 5 4 3 2 1

Chronicle Books

85 Second Street

San Francisco, California 94105

www.chroniclebooks.com

To Peggy and Pauline,

my twins

"WELL, THAT'S AGREED THEN," HE SAID, SETTLING HIMSELF INTO AN ARMCHAIR AND LIGHTING A CIGAR. "EACH OF US IS TO TELL THE STORY OF HIS FIRST LOVE. IT'S YOUR TURN FIRST, SERGEY NIKOLAICH."

Ivan Turgenev, "First Love," 1860

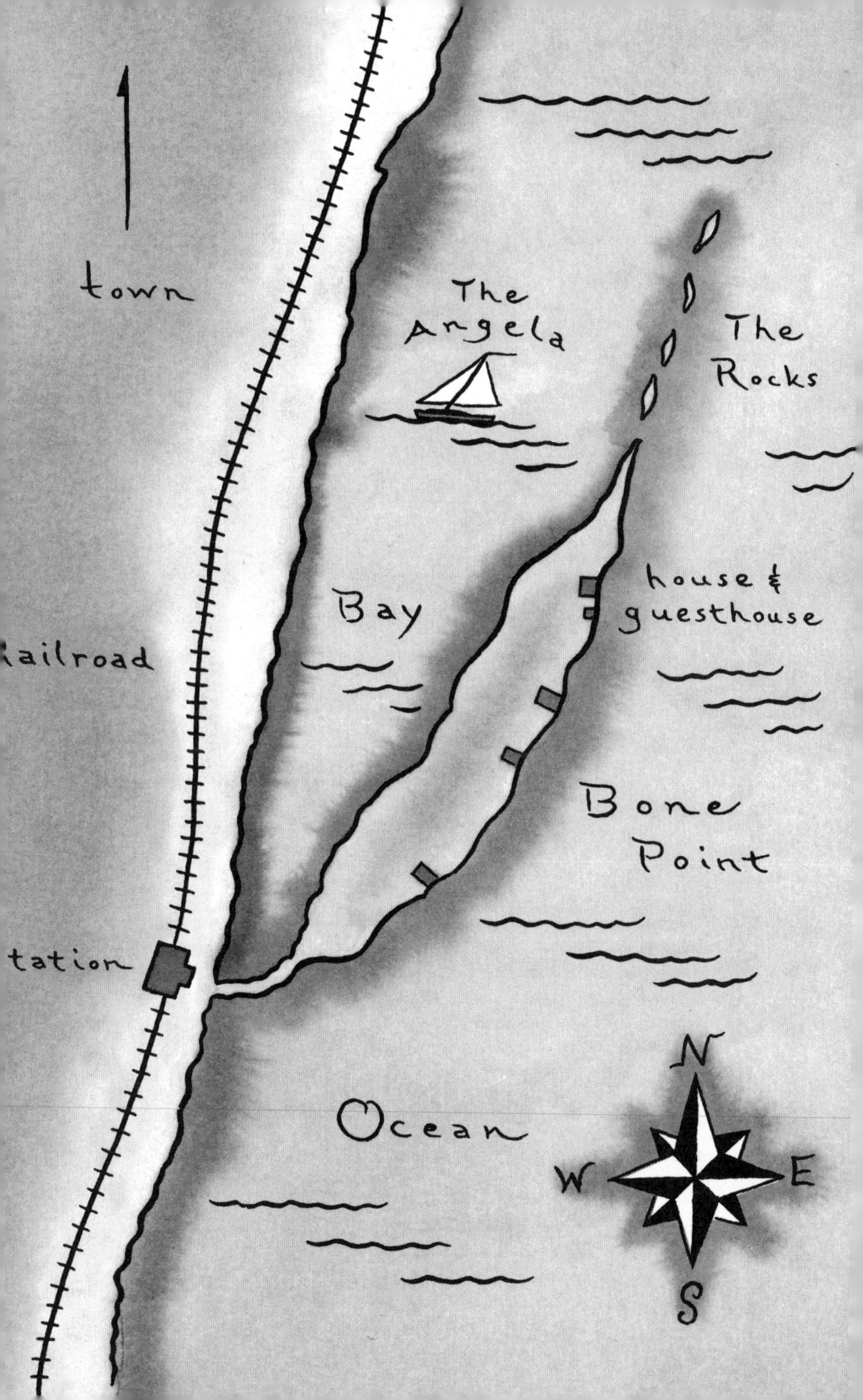
town
The Angela
The Rocks
Bay
house &
guesthouse
ailroad
Bone Point
tation
Ocean
N
W
E
S

1

The Sandbar

IN THE SUMMER of 1963 I fell in love and my father drowned.

For one week in late June a sandbar formed half a mile out in the ocean. We couldn't see it, but we knew it was there because waves were breaking on it. Each day at low tide we expected it to show through. A bar had never formed that far out, and we wondered if it would stick. If it did, the water near shore would be protected and calmer, and we could move our boat, the Angela, in front of the house instead of keeping it in Johns Bay, on the other side of Bone Point. The swimming of course would change, it would be like bay swimming, and the surf casting would be ruined.

Father and I used to fish off the shore for king, weak, blues, and bass. The bass gave the best fight and were the best eating. We pulled in a lot of sand sharks too, small, useless things we threw back. Sometimes we went for real sharks, with a big hook, too heavy to cast. We'd fix on a mackerel steak, and I'd swim out with the hook and drop it to the bottom. I did this even when I was small, except then I'd float out on my inner tube, drop the hook, and Father would pull me in with a rope. Mother didn't like this, even though we did it only when the water was calm. Once we got a hundred-pound hammerhead shark, the strangest fish I ever saw. It had a head like a sledgehammer, with eyes on the ends. People said it was a man-eater, but Father said it wasn't.

We caught stingrays too. If Father hooked one and I was up in the house, he'd shout and I'd run down with the gaff. Stingrays are broad, flat fish. When you get them near shore, in the shallow water, they can suck onto the bottom and you can't pull them in. You have to go out in high boots and work the gaff through them so that water gets in and breaks the suction. We caught rays five feet across. They have spiky tails that flail around and can give you a whack. Before you can push the gaff through the body you have to step on the tail and cut it off. They eat stingrays in some places, but we didn't.

I never went out with the gaff. Father wouldn't let me. He went out and I held the rod. Once, after Father had cut off the tail and worked the gaff through the body, the ray took off, gaff and all, and pulled me over. The reel was locked. I held onto the rod and was carried out to where Father was. He grabbed the rod from me, and by the time we got the ray in it was mostly dead. We cut it loose, and it floated out.

"Suppose I weren't here," Father said, "how long would you have held on, forever?"

"Yes," I said, and he squeezed my shoulder. I was seven that summer.

Bone Point was a special place. During World War I the government took it over for military purposes and again during World War II. After that it became a permanent federal reserve. In 1946 there were only a few houses. The agreement with the government was if you already had a house you could keep it for forty-five years, until 1991, but no new houses could be built. Mother and Father took over our house in 1948, the year I was born and the year Mother's father died. He had built the house in the early thirties, and Mother had spent her childhood summers there too.

Like me she was an only child. She claimed the house had been too big for them, just as she thought it was too big for us. Mother was a complainer. The house wasn't too big. I liked all that room and light. The first floor was full of windows and glass doors, and the porch went around the four sides. Her father had liked the light too, Mother said. She often said I reminded her of him, which pleased me because she had been so fond of him, but I felt I was more like Father. There weren't many things Father said or thought I didn't agree with.

The furniture was all from Grandfather's time, and everything was large. For instance, there was a wicker couch in the living room that Father could lie on one end of, reading, with me at the other end, and we'd only overlap from the knees down. My bedroom was big enough for my double-size bed with plenty of space left over. Blackheart, my dog, always slept with me, and we never got in one another's way. Every September we'd have to adjust when we moved back to town, where my bed was ordinary size.

Although after a week we couldn't actually see the bar, its presence got plainer every day. Complete waves were breaking on it.

"Want to swim out?" Father said.

It was as if he had read my mind.

"The tide is out," he said. "We can rest on the bar when we get there. On the way back the tide will be coming in and carry us along. What do you say?"

We were both good swimmers. Father used the crawl for general purposes. I did the backstroke, which is slower but not so tiring, and I liked looking up at the sky when I swam. Is there anything better than your body in the water and your mind in the sky? Whenever we swam together, because he was faster, Father would pull ahead, flip over, dive, stay down, come up, and fool around till I caught up. He was a regular porpoise.

I didn't think he should be doing it this time. We were heading half a mile straight out to sea, and he was using up his energy. Then two hundred yards out I knew we had miscalculated. We were moving too fast. It wasn't ebb tide, as Father had thought. The tide was still going out and speeding us to the bar. Every day the tide is an hour later. Today we had started out at noon, and I remembered that the previous day low tide had been at noon. Now low tide wouldn't be for an hour. I told Father.

"It's okay. We can wait on the bar before we swim back."

He didn't seem worried, but he didn't fool around anymore either.

When we reached the bar we found the water was deeper than we had expected. Father could stand with his mouth above water, but I couldn't. He tried holding my hand so the tide wouldn't take me farther out, but this pulled him off his feet. I had to swim just to hold my place.

"We can't rest," he said. "We'll have to go back. You mustn't panic. Do you understand?"

"I won't."

"Do you want me to help you?"

"I'll panic if you have to help me."

It was hard getting in. What kept us going was knowing that the tide against us was weakening. The question was, would the tide wear out before we did?

On the beach, figures stood watching us. As we got closer to shore and I knew we would make it I flipped over on my stomach and waved to Mother. I got a mouthful of water. Blackheart was there, along with the two people who were renting the guesthouse and their dog. It took us twenty-five minutes to get in, where it had only taken ten to get out.

Father and I lay exhausted on the beach for a long time. The two dogs sniffed us to see if we were alive. Mother held my hand. She was furious with Father. The two renters, who had just moved into the guesthouse, stayed with us. Mrs. Mertz was Mother's age. Her daughter, Zina, even upside down, was beautiful. Her eyes and hair were brown, her skin was a lighter brown, and her lips were purple. They seemed to be carved. She kept hugging and stroking her dog, as if it had been in danger instead of us. Then she touched my cheek, out of curiosity, I thought. I fell in love with Zina upside down.

After dinner that evening, Father motioned me to follow him outside. We walked to the water's edge, not saying much.

He wanted to look at the water, I thought, or get away from Mother, who wasn't speaking to him. The day had been bright and clear. Now the air was thick and damp, and a chill wind came off the ocean, turning it choppy.

"I thought for a moment out there you were going to leave me," I said.

"I wouldn't do that. Why did you think that?"

"It was just a thought."

"Would you have left me?" Father said.

"No, sir."

"Well, that's good," he said and put his arm around my shoulder. Whenever he did that I felt he loved me.

We walked back to the house. Mother was building a fire.

"Return to the scene of the crime?" she said. She was getting over it. We played Monopoly before going to bed. The wind shifted, and a nor'easter came up during the night. It lasted three days, and afterward the sandbar was gone.

2

The Photography Lesson

THE FIRST DAY after a nor'easter is sunny and cool. You can't lie on the beach, because it's still wet. If you want you can swim, but you have to know what you're doing. Father used to say that after a storm the sea is short tempered. The waves are strong and full of sand. Sand is all through the water and doesn't settle out for a couple of days. A lot of sand gets washed out from the shore, so the incline into the water is steep. An undertow can sweep you off your feet, and the gritty waves slap you down hard. Near the shore the water is unpleasant, farther out it's dangerous. Currents move against one another. Whirlpools form and pull at you.

I sat on the porch in the morning sun and thought about the renters. Father had gone into town to his office. I should warn them about the ocean. Father surely would if he were here. But I went on sitting. I couldn't understand why I just didn't get up and go over to the guesthouse and do it. There it was behind the dune, a hundred feet away. They must be up—it was ten o'clock. I suppose it was because of Zina. I was bashful about seeing her right-side up.

Renters were fairly new for us. The first time we rented was the summer before, to the Yemms. Father, who knew Mr. Yemm through business, told me he was renting the guesthouse so Mother would have company when he was in town. The trouble was Mrs. Yemm was too much company. She was always around. Also she was all over Father, which I don't think he liked, and I know Mother hated.

The Yemms had two kids, Bobby, a year older than I, and Delphine, a year younger. Bobby taught me chess. By the middle of the summer I was beating him every other game and near the end of summer all the time. He was a good sport for a while, but finally he knocked the board over, and that was our last game. I took Delphine to the sophomore prom that winter. She said she thought her mother was sweet on Father and asked me how Father felt about her mother. I said I didn't know. "I don't think they did anything," Delphine said. At the prom we both expected

she would be back this summer, but when the time came
Father told the Yemms that relatives wanted the guesthouse.
Then he rented it to Mrs. Mertz and Zina. He told me about
them before they arrived, and I asked him if the daughter
was pretty. "You'll be pleased," he said with his big smile.

I was still sitting on the porch when Zina and her dog
appeared on top of the dune. She wore a bright terry cloth
robe and was very beautiful, with her short, full, shiny brown
hair, the kind Father said a lot of butter and eggs went into,
and with her large brown eyes, serious even when she
smiled, her high cheekbones, and perfectly white teeth.
Also she had that look that said if she liked you you were
special.

"Are you going into the water?" I said.

"Do you want to?"

"You have to be careful, unless you're a very good swimmer. I was going to come over to warn you."

"Are you all recovered? I thought of swimming out to
save you."

"You'd have to be an awfully good swimmer."

"Were you scared?"

"Not after I saw we could make it."

"Was your father scared?"

"Father is never scared. He may have been scared for
me. Why did you touch my cheek like that?"

"You looked so young. I thought how sad it would be if you had drowned. What's your name?"

"Michael. I'm named for my grandfather. He died when I was born."

"What's your father's name?"

"Peter."

"Then you're Michael Petrovich." She put her finger under my chin and turned my profile. "But I'll call you Misha. My name is Zinaida Alexandrovna because my father's name is Alexander. You can call me Zina, though. I'm a casual person. This is Sonya." Her setter looked up. "She doesn't have another name, because we don't know who her father was. Nonetheless, she's a lady. How old are you?"

"Sixteen." I was fifteen.

"I'm an adult, and you're a minor, but you're a thoughtful minor, and I'll treat you accordingly."

"How much of an adult are you?"

"I'm twenty-one," she said.

Later I learned she was twenty.

"So are we going in?" she said.

"Let's do it!" I punched the sky.

Sonya stood on her hind legs and pawed the air. Blackheart appeared from nowhere, barking. Zina held back her arms, the wind blew her robe off, and the four of us ran into the water. Out beyond the tough little waves she flipped

24

forwards and backwards, dove down and shot up. She was a porpoise like Father. The water rolled off her as if she were waxed.

The dogs charged the waves. Blackheart jumped at them, bit the crests, was tumbled, righted himself, and charged again. Sonya wanted to get out to us and tried to leap over the water, but the chunky waves broke one after another and upended her. They both kept at it till we came in. Their coats were full of sand, which no amount of shaking got rid of. I was shaking too, but from a chill. Zina took my hand and hurried me up the beach. In front of the guesthouse she put her robe around me, rubbed me down, and hugged me. Then with her hands on my shoulders she kissed the tip of my nose. We were exactly the same height.

"Go behind the house!" she said. "There's no wind, and I'll bring you some medicine."

"What medicine?"

"You'll see."

Blackheart was ambling away toward home.

"Call your dog back! Now both of you, behind the house!"

The guesthouse was a frame structure Grandfather Michael had built as a combination studio and guesthouse. It was about forty feet square with cedar shingle sides and roof, two skylights, perfectly placed windows, and now a deck and shower stall out back. I remember thinking that when I got married I would bring my wife here until we could afford a place of our own.

Zina came onto the deck with a tumbler a quarter filled with clear liquid.

"Drink it down!"

It burned, as I knew it would.

"It's vodka," she said. "*Vodka* means *little water. Misha* means *little Michael.*"

She picked Blackheart up under one arm and took him into the shower stall to wash out the sand. He didn't like it, but he didn't struggle. Sonya sat by, waiting her turn. When Blackheart was done he scampered away. All Zina had to do was point, and Sonya walked under the shower and let Zina comb out the sand with her fingers. She dismissed the dog and got into the shower herself, leaving the door half open.

"Cold, oh cold!" she shouted. "Misha, this is not for you. My robe! My robe!"

I took it off and held it by the shower door. She backed out and slipped into it so quickly I didn't know whether she had her bathing suit on or not, until I saw it on the shower floor.

To my surprise—it was the vodka—I rubbed her down and gave her a hug, the way she had me. I was surprised because I really was a shy person, which I mention because she said to me with an amused look, "You're not shy, are you? All right, now you will help me with my profession."

Her camera was on the picnic table under a sun hat. She explained that she was making studies of the beach grass behind the guesthouse. I could help her by staying out of the way, particularly off the sand around the clumps of grass. She wanted it exactly as God made it, she said.

"God didn't make it. Father and I planted that grass to keep the sand from shifting."

"Nonetheless there must be no footprints."

She took pictures every which way. Straight down, alongside, circling around. She was quick and sure of herself.

"This is an exercise," she said.

I sat on the deck rail and watched her. As she bent, knelt, lay on her side or stomach, I studied her studying the grass. She kept pulling her robe together, tucking it between her legs, tightening the belt, pushing up the sleeves. She was so graceful and efficient she could have been dancing.

"These are exercises in composition," she said. "If you can make a picture of grass you can make a picture of anything."

"Do you sell your pictures?"

"Sometimes."

"Will you sell these?"

"If I like them, and somebody else likes them. Let me see that foot!"

She took my foot in her hand like a dog's paw. "You have good feet. I'll show you how I want you to place your foot. There by the grass. It's really a very nice, innocent foot, uncorrupted by shoes."

She put me next to a clump of grass and took pictures from many angles. When she finished the roll she put in another.

"I will give you a lesson." She handed me the camera. "Look through the viewfinder! Look at me! Look at the clouds! Look at the sand! No, you're looking at me. The format is two by three. Do you know what that means? Two high and three wide, like a movie. Imagine you're watching a movie. Stop looking at me! That's it. Turn the camera! That's a vertical format, three high and two wide, the portrait format. Are you following me?"

I nodded, still looking at her through the viewfinder.

"Put the camera down! These grass groups have five, ten, fifteen blades each. They describe the paths of fireworks in the sky. Do you see that? Even though the blades are curved, together they fill a square. But your camera format is rectangular. I want you to compose these square-filling things inside the camera's rectangle. You can use one bunch or more than one. You can use some of the blades in one bunch or all of them. You can use a bunch and its shadow or the shadow alone. Say something so I know you're following me!"

I was listening, but also I was looking at her so intently that I had nothing to say.

"I understand you."

She studied me for a second. "All right, you have to work fast, without thinking. You mustn't think. That's the worst thing. The eye doesn't think, it looks. But you can't just go click, click. The camera must be connected to something inside you, the way the eye is. All right, the camera is focused from here to here." She held her hands two feet apart. "Keep the camera that far from the grass. You wind the film like this. You take the picture by pushing this. Hold the camera still. You're taking still pictures." She handed me the camera. "Okay, make it see!"

I turned and took pictures of her, up and down, all sides, north, east, south, west, each picture a piece of her. She didn't move, except near the end of the roll she pushed a bent leg out from her robe in the classic bathing beauty pose.

I handed her the camera.

"Misha, you weren't photographing me, you were caressing me. Now go home! I'll show you the pictures tomorrow."

She was smiling. She liked me.

3

The Mertzes

FATHER CAME BACK from town that afternoon, and next morning we walked to the bay—Bone Point is about a mile across—to see how the Angela had weathered the storm. She's a twenty-four-foot day sailer, with a four-and-a-half-foot keel, a main and a jib sail, and a cuddy cabin that two people can sit in hunched over, or lie down in if, as Father said, they're very friendly. She was riding low. The tarp had loosened and let in rain. We bailed her out and aired the sails and while we were at it took her around the Point to the ocean.

The water was like a green bath with a shivering surface. The wind was cool, the sky pale blue, a few cloud puffs sped along. The sandbar had left no trace. We dropped anchor to twelve feet where we figured it had been.

"Full fathom two," Father said. "Who's that?" He pointed to shore.

Zina and Sonya were swimming out toward us.

"Zina Mertz."

"How can you tell?"

"That's her dog."

"We should meet them half way," Father said. "Look, the dog's turning back."

"Zina is a very good swimmer."

"How do you know?"

"I swam with her yesterday. And she's a very fine person."

That amused Father, and he gave me his big smile, which was as close as he ever came to making fun of me.

It took her forever to reach us. She was even more beautiful in the green water, with the broken, reflected sunlight flashing over her face. Father held out his hand to help her up, but she hauled herself aboard.

He asked her how she liked the guesthouse. She said she hoped he didn't mind that she had set up a darkroom. He said Grandfather Michael once had a darkroom there. "He was a passionate photographer, with absolutely no talent. Every picture was a bull's-eye. We have cartons of them. Are you a professional?"

Zina said she was, she had a group show coming up in New York in the winter, and now she was taking time off to think. "I want to do a minimum of looking for a while. This is the perfect place." She pointed to the sea. "Water and sky." She pointed to the shore. "Water, sky, and sand. Multiply that by day and night, and there are still only six things to look at. I'm cleaning out my head."

"Sounds like the French Foreign Legion," Father said.

I could see right away that he liked her. When he didn't like someone he smiled and said nothing. It was clear that she liked him too. Father was very handsome. He had fair skin, black hair, and green eyes. I used to watch when he was introduced to people. They couldn't take their eyes off him. I was very pleased he liked her. I hated it when two people I liked didn't like each other.

He told us a story about Grandfather Michael I hadn't heard before. During World War II Mother's family had to leave the Point to let the army practice beach landings. One moonless night in the summer of 1943 Grandfather made his own landing. He wanted to see how his house was doing. He came around the Point in a small sailboat, which capsized in the surf. The mast hit him on the head, and he might have drowned if a beach patrol hadn't been tracking him. They brought him to and dried him off, and the commanding officer grilled him all night, sure he was a German spy. This despite the fact that Grandfather spoke perfect American English and answered questions about Laurel and Hardy, Cole Porter, and the Boston Red Sox. The officer was almost convinced, when Grandfather offered as ultimate proof the fact that a particular burner on the stove in his house was faulty. Grandfather forgot that he had put the stove in the basement. As a result, the officer sent Grandfather under guard to an intelligence center in Virginia, where he was kept incommunicado and interrogated for two days. He was finally released with a mild apology and a strong reprimand.

Father managed the mainsail and tiller, and we sailed along parallel to the shore. Zina and I shifted from side to side as we came about. Each time, she pinched my arm, which thrilled me.

"My father was born in Germany," she said. "He was brought up there, but he's an American. He came here with his parents after the war. His father, my grandfather, was a famous scientist. Did you ever hear of Victor Mertz? There's a town in Alabama named Mertz."

I knew what Father was going to say. "Michael was born in Germany. I was doing business there in the late forties. We came back when my father-in-law died. I believe Michael can apply for German citizenship."

"Fat chance," I said.

"Misha is completely American," Zina said.

"Why do you call him Misha then?"

"It's my favorite name, and he is now one of my favorite people. As for you, you're even more American."

"Somehow," Father said, "that doesn't sound like a compliment."

"We can't help being what we are, and what I meant about Misha is he's easier to understand than European boys. Do you mind that, Misha?"

"I mind the boy part."

"European *males*."

"How about the rest of you," Father said, "besides the German part?"

"The rest is Russian," she said and explained that her mother's parents left Russia after the revolution and joined the Russian colony in Paris. "My mother was born there. Strictly speaking, she's a princess."

"How about you?" Father said.

"Me too," she said and dove into the water. She came up and swam toward shore.

"She knows how to make an exit," Father said.

We tacked behind her at a discreet distance until she reached the beach.

After lunch I was sitting on the porch with Blackheart when Zina appeared on the dune and waved us over. She took us around to the deck and showed me a dozen of her grass pictures. They were black-and-white and, except for the foot pictures, seemed more like drawings than photographs. The one I liked best was of a single clump with seven blades. Those that bent toward and away from the camera were almost vertical lines. Those bending sideways had the fullest curves. No blade crossed any other. I told her I liked this one best.

"Why?"

"It's the simplest. But they're all good."

"Why?"

"They're tense and peaceful."

"I love you," she said. She pulled my head forward and kissed my nose. "Now here are your pictures." On cardboard she had pasted the snapshots—each was an inch by an inch and a half—one above the other in four groups. The images didn't mesh, but there she was, opened up and flattened out, two side views, one front view, one back.

"You've reinvented cubism," she said. "I'm very impressed."

When I didn't say anything, she said, "I really am impressed, Misha."

"I just preferred taking pictures of you than of grass."

"Nonetheless you are a darling boy—darling male."

Sonya appeared, and Blackheart tried to mount her.

"Stop!" I yelled.

"Oh, let him! A lady likes to be asked."

I was not only embarrassed generally, I was embarrassed for Blackheart, who was half as tall as the setter. He yipped and whined and leaped to reach her. She didn't even look around to see what was happening.

"Talk about a flying fuck," Mrs. Mertz said through the screen door.

"Mother, come out! This is Misha. You met him on the beach, the drowned rat, and that's his dog. I don't give him much chance, do you?"

"They don't seem suited," Mrs. Mertz said and came onto the deck with a drink in her hand. The three of us sat down. Mrs. Mertz caught Blackheart's attention, and he gave the setter up. I could see from the way the setter folded her paws beneath her and took her place among us that she considered herself somebody. Like the setter, Mrs. Mertz had reddish-brown hair and her arms and legs were long and fashionable. Also like the setter she tucked her bare feet under her. She told Zina to bring me something to drink. Without asking what I wanted, Zina brought me another vodka, which she gave me with a giggle. Mrs. Mertz was paler and thinner than Zina. As I sipped the vodka, I subtracted Mrs. Mertz from Zina to see if I could picture what the father was like. Strong and dark, I thought. I told Mrs. Mertz my formula and asked if I was right.

"Absolutely. You *are* clever."

"What does Mr. Mertz do?" I said.

"God only knows. I haven't heard from him for months. Have you, Zina?"

"One letter."

"Well, what *is* he doing?"

"The usual thing."

"Well, there you are, Misha. Zina's father is doing the usual thing."

I didn't finish the vodka and after an hour left with my pasted-up pictures.

4

The Porch Party

SUNDAY MORNING FATHER, Mother, Zina, and I sailed from Johns Bay to town and the Church of the Fishers of Men. It had an arrangement with a nearby marina to park the boats of parishioners during services. Mrs. Mertz said she would stay on the Point and worship the sun god. Zina really didn't belong in her gauzy flowered dress and floppy brimmed hat. She seemed to be playing the part of going to church on Sunday. In fact when we were pulling into the marina she said, "Misha, pinch me if I giggle."

Mr. Walton liked to use aquatic themes in his sermons. This one was called "The Personal Deluge" and was about "those times that come to all of us when seemingly endless trouble rains upon us. Then it is that we must cleave to our loved ones, hold fast to our faith in deliverance, and wait, if need be, through forty days and forty nights for the flood of affliction to subside."

Mr. Walton was famous for his wife, Elaine, the most beautiful woman in town. Father said that if Mr. Walton used her for bait he would be a truly great fisher of men. He also said that since we could go to church only in good weather that the matter of attendance was in God's hands and we should not feel guilty on gusty Sundays. Zina said, I think seriously, that during the service she had thought of a way to photograph God.

As we did that Sunday, we sometimes sailed around the Point and anchored in front of the house. Since we had no dock on the oceanside, we'd strip down to our underwear and wade ashore, holding our clothes above our heads. I was always a little embarrassed to see Mother in bra and panties, even though there was more to her underwear than to her bathing suit. This was always fun, and it was good to see Mother in a happy mood.

I was surprised when Father decided to sail around the Point that Sunday. Had he forgotten about Zina? He carried her ashore. Her hat came off and got wet, and so did the hem of her dress. Father looked like a groom carrying his bride over the threshold. We were laughing so much—

Mother most of all—we could hardly walk through the water.

Mother had mixed feelings about summers at Bone Point. It was one of the important places of her childhood. On the other hand, she didn't like "being abandoned," as she described Father's business trips to town. And even when he was at the Point he seemed to spend more time alone or with me than with Mother. That was one of the reasons she liked giving parties. We usually had one in July—this one today— one in August, and wound up the season with the Labor Day party in September.

After lunch Father and I sailed south along the shore past the base of the Point to a little beach village on the mainland with a famous cheese store. While Father shopped, Blackheart and I kept the Angela pointed into the wind, the sails flapping and snapping. It sounded like complaining, and when Father waded out with the cheese he said the Angela didn't like doing errands, she was a lady.

"Zina said her dog is a lady."

"Setters are jumpy and dumb. A lady cannot be jumpy and dumb. A lady is serene and always knows what others are thinking."

"Is Mother a lady?"

"Pretty much."

"Is Mrs. Mertz a lady?"

41

"I interviewed her, not to see if she was a lady, but to see if she was respectable."

"Is she?"

"Respectable enough. We'll see at the party if she's a lady."

"Do you think she's attractive?"

"Quite attractive."

"But Zina is beautiful."

"Quite beautiful," Father said with his big smile.

Sailing back, I was very happy. There I was, in the Angela with Father and Blackheart. The sky was a deep, cloudless blue. If I looked far enough I could see the night beyond it. And, besides that, at five o'clock Zina and her mother would be at the party. The Cuddihys were sailing down from the mainland. Mother had gone to school with Mrs. Cuddihy and was always in a good mood when she was around. Mr. Cuddihy was a builder. I think Father and he did business together. We sailed the Angela around to the bay and walked across the Point to the house. The porch had a sunny side and a shady side, a lee side and a windward side, a dry side and a wet side. It was a perfect place to read, nap, or have a party.

The Cuddihys arrived on time. Mrs. Cuddihy and Mother kissed and embraced. Father and Mr. Cuddihy shook hands and made themselves drinks. Father never drank before a party, and Mr. Cuddihy never didn't. He was a big man. His face was always red. He had big hands and feet, and everybody liked him, including me, except when he said things like, "Michael, Michael, when are you going to catch up with your dad? You haven't got all that much time. Come here and say hello to Melissa."

The Cuddihys made out that their daughter, Melissa, and I were going together. Actually we only saw one another when our parents met. Melissa was a nice girl and not bad looking, and she liked poetry, which I did too. What kept me from enjoying her more was that she was two inches taller than I was. That Sunday she brought me the poems of Edna St. Vincent Millay.

My parents and the Cuddihys were laughing and drinking, and Melissa was reading me a Millay sonnet, which I could tell she knew by heart:

> What lips my lips have kissed, and where, and why
> I have forgotten, and what arms have lain
> Under my head till morning. . . .

Someone suddenly turned, and the rest of us looked. Zina and her mother were climbing the dune in front of the guesthouse, appearing head first, then shoulders, and so on. "Venus rising," Father said. I wondered which one he meant.

Mrs. Mertz was dressed in a black blouse and white slacks, Zina in yellow slacks and an orange blouse.

As they came toward us, the strangest notion occurred to me, that Mrs. Mertz was more beautiful than Zina. Mrs. Mertz walked, not like a princess, but like a queen, straight, looking directly at us, smiling a little. And then, probably intending to, she threw it all away by dragging on a cigarette. Zina was a few steps behind, looking down. The two of them made such an impression that it took us a few minutes to absorb them.

There were now eight of us on the porch in two groups, like a ballet. Father and Mr. Cuddihy enjoying themselves with Zina and Mrs. Mertz; Mother, standing with Mrs. Cuddihy, Melissa, and me. Mother couldn't concentrate on what was being said. I knew what was on her mind. Whenever Father was having a good time with a pretty woman like Mrs. Mertz Mother was impelled to do something about it. She had worked up a stock of moves. She would join Father and inject herself into the conversation; she would send him on an errand; she would call him away to introduce him to someone. Father knew what she was up to because there'd always be that big smile. But he'd go along. I once asked him if Mother was the jealous type. "More the careful type," he said.

The problem for Mother now was that Mrs. Cuddihy was bringing her up to date on their college classmates, and the news was endless. The best Mother could do was stand so that she could watch Father. I watched too. Zina was giving Mr. Cuddihy her full attention, and Mrs. Mertz was telling Father a story. He was either amused or making out he was. Melissa was trying to break me away from our mothers. To avoid this I left the group and took up a position between Mrs. Mertz and Zina. Mrs. Mertz retold the beginning of her story for my benefit. It seems her husband was once cutting grass with a big stand-behind mower. The blade picked up a piece of copper wire and shot it into Mr. Mertz's stomach. Mrs. Mertz drove him to the hospital, where an emergency operation was performed by an émigré, Moscow-trained surgeon. A week after he left the hospital Mr. Mertz went to the Russian surgeon's office for an examination. Mr. Mertz said in passing, "I may not be able to cut the grass, but I can still cut the mustard."

"What is 'cut mustard'?" the surgeon said.

"Fuck."

"Fuck, you can't fuck. You open stomach."

"I did it on my side," Mr. Mertz said.

"Oh, on your side," the surgeon said and shrugged.

"So, since then," Mrs. Mertz said, "I've felt if you do it on your side it doesn't count."

The men were amused, although Mr. Cuddihy looked as if he wasn't sure the story should be told in front of me. No doubt Zina had heard it before.

With a conspiratorial look Zina left and joined the other group. By the time I could follow her she and Melissa were off by themselves. Melissa was in shorts and sandals. She wasn't so much heavy as big. Her knees had indentations. She was doing the talking.

"You are obviously the graphic type. Michael and I are verbal types. We like images all right, but when it comes to expressing ourselves we do it in words. Now here's a test for the verbal type. Butterflies flutter by. If you think that's pure magic you're the verbal type. If it's just words you're not. There's a difference, though, between Michael and me." She put her hand on my arm. "You can deny it if you like, Michael, but the fact is I *think*, then *say*; Michael *says*, then *thinks*."

At the moment I was doing the opposite. I was saying nothing, but I certainly was thinking. What was she doing? I had never heard this kind of nervous chattering out of her. She was talking as if we were an item. I had never touched one part of her person. I had never even taken her out. Where was this coming from?

Then suddenly Mr. Cuddihy was beside us. "Honey, is that wine you're drinking?"

"Mother said I could."

"Just one. How about you?" he said to Zina. "Can I get you something?"

"I'll come with you," Zina said.

46

I was furious with Melissa. "What was all that about, me talking first, you thinking first?"

"You do."

"You don't *know* me well enough to know that. You don't know me at *all*." I was losing my breath.

"Why are you getting angry? I was only trying to pay you a compliment."

"What compliment?"

"That you're spontaneous."

"Oh, for Christ's sake!"

She looked ready to cry.

"All right, Melissa. I'm not angry. It's just that I don't think you know what you're talking about."

"You didn't want me talking about you to Zina. That's it isn't it?"

"That *isn't* it."

"You like her."

"Melissa, everyone likes Zina. Your father likes Zina. Look, he's all over her."

Melissa spun around and walked off the porch toward the beach. Mother was watching us and knew something was up. She nodded for me to follow Melissa. I didn't want to, but I did. I caught up with her, and we strolled along the beach. I took her hand. I didn't want to, but I did. By the time we returned to the house she was okay.

Everyone had moved to the ocean porch to see the sunset. As the top of the sun went below the horizon Mr. Cuddihy said, "Going . . . going . . . *gone*," and everyone cheered.

We ate inside. The people who had been drinking liquor switched to wine. After the food Mr. Cuddihy played tunes on the piano. We gathered around and sang along. Zina went onto the porch and called Sonya. She loped over, was nuzzled by Zina, and settled down outside. Blackheart barked, and we bribed him with a dish of shrimp. Melissa turned out to have a pretty voice. So did Mrs. Mertz. After some songs—"Just One of Those Things," "Night and Day," "Stormy Weather"—she recited the lyrics in French as Mr. Cuddihy touched the appropriate chords.

"Your mother's terrific," I whispered to Zina.

"That girl's in love with you," she whispered back.

"I'm not in love with her."

"You have a responsibility to someone who loves you."

I didn't know what to say to that, but if I told her I loved *her* would she have a sense of responsibility to me?

"She gave you a book of poems. You give her something back."

"All right."

"Something that means something to you."

"All right."

But I didn't. I went to my room for the copy of Yeats's poems that Melissa had given me on another occasion, and I inscribed it "For Zina, page 114," which had a line Yeats said he found in an old play:

In dreams begins responsibility.

I gave her the book in the dark as she stood on the sand with her mother, thanking us at the end of the party.

5

The Day After

NEXT MORNING I had breakfast with Mother. Father was working on the Angela.

Mother could look older or younger. She looked younger when she was in a bad mood; she moved quickly, and her face was thinner. When she was in a good mood she looked plump, and her movements were round; she put objects down in a kind of curve and walked from one place to another in an arc. This morning she was in a good mood, and she talked about the party, which meant it had been a success.

Mary Cuddihy was a "dear woman," particularly because "as time goes by it's hard to make new friends and impossible to make old ones." Mrs. Cuddihy reminded Mother that for a semester they had called each other Charmian and Iras after two of Cleopatra's handmaidens. "Cleopatra was Peebee Brooks, who taught us Elizabethan literature. I had completely forgotten that."

About Melissa, "She'll be just fine as soon as she grows up a little."

"You don't mean physically," I said.

"She does take after her father, doesn't she. As for Zina, she's intelligent and well-behaved."

"And beautiful," I said.

"She has an interesting face, and she really listens to what you're saying. I like that in a person."

"How about Mrs. Mertz? Is she well-behaved? Do you think she's a lady?"

"She could pass in some crowds. Your father probably thinks she is."

"But you don't."

"She's female, that's for sure. And Blackheart is too excitable. We should have had him fixed when we could."

"Father is against fixing."

"Your father is a natural-state romantic."

"Me too."

"You're a romantic about women, Michael."

"Is Father?"

She paused and then said, "I don't know."

After breakfast I went to the bay. Father was checking the mooring chain for rust. He was especially handsome when he was intent on something. He was really not like a father at all, at least as far as discipline went. Mother was the one who told me what I could and couldn't do. Father told me what I should and shouldn't do.

The tide was low, the water waist high beside the boat. I helped Father feed the chain aboard and asked him what he thought of the party. He said it was fun and asked me what I thought.

"Okay. What do you think of Mrs. Mertz now?"

"Life of the party, along with Frank Cuddihy."

"Mother thinks you like her."

"Did she say that?"

"Sort of."

"Everybody likes her." Exactly my words about Zina.

"Not Mother," I said

"Did she say so?"

"No, but I can tell. You like Zina, don't you?"

"Zina is not a simple girl, Michael."

"Who thinks she's simple?"

"You do. You think she's perfect. Perfect is very simple."

"You once said to me that ordinary women stay near shore, extraordinary women swim out. Zina is extraordinary, isn't she?"

"Well, she does swim out."

As we got back to the house we saw a cabin cruiser anchored in the ocean a hundred feet off shore, new and shiny, bobbing and tilting. Father and I were snobbish about power boats. Our feeling was, you might as well take a drive on the highway as sail a power boat. In a sailboat you hear and feel and smell only wind and water. You're doing what people did thousands of years ago. Take the Angela. She was made of wood and cloth, like sailboats always. She enjoyed the ocean as much as the bay. She was a dreamer and rode so easily she turned you into a dreamer. Who dreams on a power boat? On a power boat you have ambitions, not dreams. The Angela liked to be pushed, but didn't do tricks. She preferred a strong and steady wind, but smoothed out gusts, never got upset, and was perfectly happy to idle along in a breeze. If you didn't always know what you were doing she forgave you. She was heavy for her size and preferred not to race. Father said if she were a woman she'd have had big breasts and buttocks, been a better mother than wife, and a better wife than mistress.

There seemed to be no one on the cruiser. At first we thought the visitors would be in our house, but over her shoulder Mother pointed to the guesthouse. "Two exquisite males," she said, "bronzed and up for a lark."

Because of the dune I couldn't see them, but I could

hear them. Father wasn't interested, and I tried not to be. Were they Zina's friends or her mother's? I thought of returning to the Angela, but there was nothing more to do there. I thought of challenging Father to a game of chess, but he had already spread out on the north porch, reading. Finally I motioned to Blackheart, and we hopped over the hot sand to the guesthouse. On the way I plucked a blade of grass to chew and be a casual person, like Zina.

Zina and her mother were glad to see us. Mrs. Mertz, in a bikini, kissed my cheek. Zina took my hand and introduced me to the guests. Henry ran an art gallery in town. Wilder, younger, was a photographer. Henry had a black tan and blond hair. He stood straight and shook my hand seriously. Wilder was friendly too, but not so formal.

Zina told them how I had rediscovered cubism with my photographs of her. Mrs. Mertz hadn't heard about them, and I promised to bring them over. Henry said that he had immediately seen that I was creative and that I could have sat for Egon Schiele, I was that "innocent and knowing."

"Henry," Mrs. Mertz said, "stop the bullshit! You're embarrassing Misha."

Henry asked me if I was really Russian, and Mrs. Mertz said I should stay for lunch.

During the meal there was a lot of talk about Bone Point. It was just the place for Mrs. Mertz—nothing to worry about. I got the impression she was recuperating from something, although she looked perfectly healthy, except thin. There was also a lot of talk about photography. I guess they thought I would be interested. I didn't recognize any of the names. One of the photographers specialized in nudes. Was his work pornographic?

Mrs. Mertz said it was as arousing as a clothespin.

"Women," Henry said, "are notoriously insensitive to visual stimuli."

Zina said the pictures were "too three dimensional—nude Karshes."

She could see I wasn't very interested and put her hand over mine to console me. This didn't seem to bother anyone. Did it mean neither Henry nor Wilder was interested in Zina, or was I too young to be competition? By age Henry should have belonged to Mrs. Mertz, and Wilder to Zina. But I supposed it could just as well be the other way around.

After lunch we swam out to the cruiser, which was named the Chelsea Hotel. For half an hour Henry sped her up and down along the shore and out to sea and back. He was showing off and pushed her to thirty knots, churning up a great wake. He invited me to take the wheel and from behind held my hands as I steered. Power boats are fun for a while, but they're too easy. Anyone can run a power boat with two minutes instruction—just don't hit anything.

After that we settled on the guesthouse deck. Mrs. Mertz took orders for drinks, played a Nina Simone record, and sang along. Henry asked her to dance and immediately picked up a splinter. Mrs. Mertz brought out needle and tweezers and offered to remove it, but Henry said he wanted "a young, firm hand," me. Actually I'm pretty good with splinters. We sat down on facing chairs, and I took his foot in my lap. I was poking around when suddenly Henry said, "Oh, my God, the pain! Don't stop!"

I didn't understand he was joking until I saw everyone was laughing, including Henry.

Suddenly Father was there, still in his bathing trunks. I suppose he had heard the music and general jollity. Mrs. Mertz put an arm around his bare back, as if he were a dear old friend, and introduced him as "the best-looking land-lord in memory." She asked Father if he wanted a drink, and when she came out with it, and one for herself, she asked him to dance. That was the scene when Mother ar-rived—Father and Mrs. Mertz, each holding a drink in their left hand, his right hand around her waist, hers on his shoulder.

Mother was something else when she was angry. Mrs. Mertz let Father go and tried to introduce Mother to Henry and Wilder. Mother nodded to each in turn but wouldn't take either's hand. With a shake of her head she refused

Mrs. Mertz's offer of a drink. She didn't sit when Mrs. Mertz asked her to, and she stepped away from Father when he came near her. To finish it off, Blackheart, who also had showed up, started sniffing Sonya's behind and crooning. Mother gave him an awful whack. He yipped and scurried off. Father winked at me. Mrs. Mertz had retreated against the wall of the guesthouse and was taking it all in over the edge of her drink. Zina stared at the deck floor. Henry and Wilder looked confused. Mother, who was extra angry for having lost her temper with Blackheart, had the sense to leave. Through it all she hadn't said a word.

"I hope your wife . . . ," Mrs. Mertz said. Father held up his hand. In the same motion he indicated that I should hang around for a while and went back to the house.

"Well," Mrs. Mertz said with a sigh and a smile, "shall we dance?"

No one wanted to.

Henry and Wilder said they had to get back.

Mrs. Mertz said she was going to take a nap.

"The trouble is," Zina said when everyone was gone, "Mother has one drink and she thinks she's Brigitte Bardot."

"The trouble is my father likes Brigitte Bardot."

"I hope you didn't mind Henry's camping around. He's really not like that."

"How is he really?"

"He's been the best friend to Mother. When Father walked out she fell apart. Henry saved her life."

"You must like him a lot."

"I do. All right, your father's had time to make peace. Now go home and tell your funny little dog to mind his manners."

Instead I walked to the bay and stood at the water's edge. Blackheart showed up. We liked the low-tide stench of the sea-plant rot. The late afternoon sun had turned the sky violet. The Angela, unmoving in the glassy water, was the perfect boat. Blackheart was the best and most loyal dog in the world. Talking to Zina about her mother and my father made me feel closer to her. It was almost as if we had conspired.

As I got back to the house, Father was walking off toward the ocean.

I went upstairs. The door of my parents' bedroom was shut. I knocked.

"Go away!" Mother said.

"It's me."

"You too."

Blackheart followed me downstairs and watched carefully. Either he wanted an explanation or dinner. I fed him, and he wandered off.

I didn't know which way Father was walking. If north, toward the end of the Point, he would be back soon. If south, toward the mainland, he might never come back.

The parents of my closest friend, Hillyer, had split two years ago. He was pretty depressed at first. He felt they should have waited till he and his kid brother were grown. I had just gotten a letter from him. His father was in South America, and his brother wasn't talking to his mother. "There ought to be a better way of getting into the world than having parents," he wrote.

This would not happen to our family, I thought. Father knew how to handle Mother. He could always bring her around. He'd give her a hug, and she'd frown. He'd give her another hug, and she'd smile. Mother adored him.

However, if Father did fall in love with Mrs. Mertz, would they actually live together? It was hard to imagine Father living with Mrs. Mertz. She was attractive, even beautiful, but she needed a lot of attention of the kind Father didn't give out. In a way she was like Father. They were both charmers, except he was an amateur, she was in the business.

So how would they get along? He would probably be lively and talkative, and so would she. Or maybe with a different kind of wife he would be quiet and let her talk. I pictured Zina and me exchanging looks at things they said to each other. But whatever happened between them Zina would remain my stepsister. Or would she? Those were my thoughts as I waited for Father to get back.

He walked in as I was rummaging through the refrigerator.

"Any news from upstairs?"

"Maybe we should go up and see," I said.

"Let's fix something to eat, and I'll take it up."

We made sandwiches. Father put two on a tray with glasses and a bottle of wine. He held the tray on his hand above his head and mounted the stairs like an actor playing a waiter.

He came right down. "I left it outside the door. Where's Blackheart?"

"Asleep on the porch."

"He's partial to sandwiches."

"Did Mother lock the door?"

"Yup, but I have a plan. Let's eat first."

"What did you think of those visitors?" I said.

"You were on their boat. What did you think?"

"They were okay. Do you think they're interested in Zina and Mrs. Mertz?"

"Romantically, no."

"Why not?"

"That's just what I think."

His plan worked. We took the ladder from under the east porch, put it against the house, and he climbed through the bedroom window. Mother screamed, but before long she was laughing. He really was an expert. I wondered if I'd ever be able to do that with women.

6

A Warning

NEXT MORNING THE sky was pale blue and cloudless, the ocean green and clear near shore and blue-black far out. A snappy breeze blew in from the bay over the Point and into the sea, keeping the water smooth and the breaking waves small and tight. It was a nifty day for sailing.

There were four houses on the Point if you count our house and the guesthouse as one. The house nearest the mainland was a snug little shack belonging to Mr. Strangfeld, who had been living there alone since before World War II. The older he got the more we wondered how he managed in the winter. He had electricity but no phone. If he had gotten into trouble, there wouldn't have been much he could do about it. Every spring when we opened the house we half expected to hear that he had died, his flesh stripped by rats.

He made his living from the Pointers. He drove his beach buggy past the house every morning about eight. If we wanted a ride to the mainland we planted a green flag in the sand and he picked us up. It was the only way to get off the Point by land. He did it rain or shine as long as anyone was left. He performed two other services. We all had wells, but the water was brackish. Mr. Strangfeld delivered ten-gallon bottles of drinking water from the mainland. When we wanted one we left the empty in front of the house and he changed it for a full one. Also, he kept an eye on the houses during the winter to see they hadn't been burgled, blown down, or washed away. I don't know how much we Pointers paid him, but it was enough for his taxes, electricity, and food. We could have had our own beach buggies, but we felt to deny Mr. Strangfeld any part of his income would have endangered his survival.

Bone Point stretches six miles north-south along the mainland, with the end of the Point to the north, the ocean on the east, and the bay on the west. By Grandfather Michael's day Bone Point was an island, but it must have been a peninsula once, when it was named. During World War II the Army Engineers built a causeway from the southern end to the mainland. The town, with a population then of seventy thousand, was about three miles to the north. What Mr. Strangfeld did was drive us to the base of the Point, over the causeway to the mainland, where you could take the coastal rail line one stop into the center of town. We kept our car at the station and usually drove into town alongside the railroad.

Father went in that morning, so I gathered up my courage and invited Zina to sail. She was so beautiful in her candy-striped bathing suit that it made me self-conscious to look at her. I put her in charge of the mainsail, and she learned quickly. In no time she was ducking and shifting like a veteran. I told her she would make a good sailor, which got us talking about what we wanted to be.

She wanted to be a good photographer, "not famous, just good." She explained that she hadn't yet plotted her course, mainly because of what she called the chrome shift, the change from black-and-white to color. She said that color photography had been technically perfected too soon. "Black-and-white had years to go. Now it's hard to resist color. Plenty of serious photographers do only black-and-white, but there's something affected about it, like making black-and-white movies. Color may never be any good, it may be too real. Good photographs aren't real, they're pictures of what you think about what's real." She said the truth had come to her one evening in a New York restaurant. "There were black-and-whites on the wall. Everything else was in color. I was in color, the man opposite me, the chairs, the floor. The pictures were the only exception, the only refuge. Art is a refuge from reality."

She asked me if I had a talent. I said I thought I had a talent for happiness. "Like Father," I added.

She said I seemed more serious than Father.

"Father is very serious. It doesn't show, because he's witty and he's nice to people."

"You're nice to people, Misha, when you want to be."

I knew what she was getting at, which I didn't want to talk about, so I said, "But do you think I have a talent for happiness?"

"I think you have a talent for goodness."

"What good is that?"

"It's good for the people around you."

"Is it good for you?" I said.

"Maybe. But when I said you were nice to people when you wanted to be—"

"You meant Melissa."

"That girl loves you."

"I don't love her."

"If I were a man," Zina said, "I'd make love to every woman who loved me."

"Suppose you were a movie actor and thousands of women loved you."

"I'd make love to every one of them once. It would be my sacred obligation."

"What about when they wanted to do it again?" I said.

"I'd explain about my sacred obligation to the others and send them away."

"Suppose they insisted?"

"I'd tell them they were lucky to get me once."

"What would you do if I said I loved you?"

"Well, Misha, I'm not a man. A woman must love a man before she makes love with him. That's *her* sacred obligation."

"Well, I love you."

"Maybe you do, and maybe you don't. I'll give you a test. Can I let go of this sail?"

I turned the Angela into the wind, and Zina sat down beside me. "All right," she said, "I will kiss you on the eyes, but you must keep them open."

"Kiss me on the actual eyes?"

"Yes, and if you can't keep them open you don't love me."

"I can do it."

"You can't keep them open with your fingers."

"I know. Go ahead!"

67

She touched one eye with the tip of her tongue. She let me close my eyes in between. Then she touched the other eye. Tears ran down my face.

"You're really crying," she said

"I really love you," I said.

She dove into the water. I could handle that mainsail and the tiller perfectly well myself, but to take over so suddenly flustered me. She came right to the surface. We were far out, and she was surprised by the feel of deep water. It has a swell and pull that let you know you're in its power. The sails caught the wind and the Angela moved away. Struggling to get the boat under control, I saw on Zina's face not fear so much as intense curiosity. I wanted to get to her before she became afraid.

Returning to a given spot in a sailboat is not easy. You don't move in a circle, as you would in a power boat. You execute a figure eight. As roundabout as that sounds, it's the proven way to get back to someone overboard. Father taught it to me. I had done it once, and did it again now. Zina at first thought I was sailing away from her. I kept shouting, "It's okay. I'm coming back."

She needed help getting aboard. We didn't talk much going in. She had been afraid.

After we moored I asked her if she would have lunch with Mother and me.

"You better see if your mother would like that."

"My mother was peeved with your mother, not with you."

Mother said sure, and I fetched Zina from the guest-house.

I loved listening to the two of them. They brought out the lady in each other. They talked as if I weren't there.

Zina wanted to know what Father did (he was an insurance broker with his own business), where we lived in the winter (in an apartment in town), whether Mother or Father had been married before (no), whether Mother had more women friends than men friends (women), whether Mother had a job or profession (no).

Zina said she knew she would be a success as a photographer.

Mother asked how she knew.

"Because I want it so much."

"Do you think things work that way?" Mother said.

"In my case," Zina said and smiled, and Mother laughed.

Zina said she had been born in New York City, which she liked because it was "half European." She went to college for only one year because she had thought she wanted to be a philosopher, but it turned out that she was more interested in things than ideas. She liked Bone Point because she didn't have to wear shoes. Her parents had been living apart for six years but were still married. Mr. Mertz was in import/export and traveled a lot. Zina didn't plan to marry for a while, if ever, and if she had children she would wait till she was thirty at least. She had more men friends than women friends, which she intended to change, "because there's more to learn from women; men only teach you about themselves." She knew she was attractive to men, but that was because she was independent. "Men like independent women. They're easy to get rid of when the time comes."

"I doubt you learned that from experience," Mother said.

Zina giggled. "Really my mother said that, I didn't."

I was very pleased that Mother liked her. I wanted everyone I loved to be close. Mother, Father, Zina, Blackheart. And maybe there was room for Mrs. Mertz.

As she was leaving, Zina said, "I think you have a peach of a kid."

"So does your mother," Mother said.

"I would like to say . . . I want you to know . . . Mother is really harmless. Would you come and have lunch with us?"

"I'd love to."

I admired how quickly Mother said it.

Zina kissed Mother's cheek, touched the tip of my nose with her finger, and left.

We cleared the table silently. I was sure Mother would have something to say, but she didn't. So finally I said,

"Zina's okay, isn't she?"

"Yes, she is," Mother said, turning away.

"Do you think she'll be a success?"

"If she doesn't lose her way."

"How could she do that?"

"Get married and have kids and give up a career. Any number of ways."

"She said she'll be a success because she wants it so much."

Mother turned around angrily. "She's wrong. She may be a success, or she may not, but it won't be because she wants it. Life is not like that. Don't you understand that?"

"No, I don't."

"Michael, Zina may look like a girl to you, but she is a grown woman. She will break your heart if you don't get this idea out of your head. You do not get in life what you want because you want it, you get what life gives you."

She went out to the porch, slamming the door behind her.

7

A Trip to Town

I WENT TO town the day Mother had lunch with Mrs. Mertz
and Zina. Mr. Strangfeld drove me to the station. He was
perfectly American as far as I could tell, but he knew I had
been born in Germany, and he liked to use German phrases
with me, *guten Morgen, guten Tag, wie gehts*. When he
picked me up that morning I said, "It sure is a fantastic *Morgen* this *Morgen*." "*Ach, ja*," he said, "*sehr schön*," which he
translated for me: "Oh, yes, very beautiful." And it was
beautiful—cool and crisp and clear.

The town, Father said, was just the right size, small enough
to know what's going on, but not so small it didn't have mys-
teries. Rich people moved in at the beginning of the century.

One of them built the college, and another built the art museum. People liked it because it didn't have mills or factories.

My pal Hillyer, the one whose parents were divorced, was coming from his country place to meet me. He wanted to go on a movie binge—one in the morning, two in the afternoon. I wanted to go to the museum. Zina had been talking about the impressionists ("they painted light, not things"), and I wanted to fill my head with what was in her head, although I didn't try to explain this to Hillyer. We compromised. We did the museum in the morning, then after lunch we saw the flick the museum was showing and another one in a regular movie house.

My main reason for going to town was to have dinner with Father. Mother had suggested it, and I always enjoyed it. Hillyer's reason was to spend the night with his girlfriend. He had described in his letter how he had come into town and tried it a couple of weeks before, but when they opened the door of his house some lights were on. Had his father come home from South America? Hillyer left the girlfriend at the corner and went back to investigate. The house had been broken into. He tried to persuade her to come back with him ("We can call the police later"), but she was too shook up and he walked her home. It had taken a lot of effort to get her to try again. He promised to go through the place first to make sure the coast was clear.

The paintings were great, except there weren't enough of them. I bought some Monet waterscape postcards as a memento. The museum movie was an old French flick *Devil in the Flesh*, about a boy who was having an affair with the new wife of a soldier away fighting in World War I. It was as if the movie had been chosen for me. The second one was *Lolita*. Hillyer pointed out that both couples had an age gap. I secretly thought this was a good omen for me, even though the movies ended unhappily.

I wished Hillyer luck with his girl and went on to Bobo's Steakhouse, a roomy, oaken place. Along the bar there were dice in leather cups the customers threw to see who would pay for drinks. The captain recognized me and said that Father had called. If I arrived first I was to be seated, a bottle of red wine was to be put on the table, and if, when no one was looking, I were to help myself, what could the law do about it? I was on my second glass when Father showed up.

I saw him as soon as he came in. So did everyone else. He was in black tie. The captain took him by the hand and elbow; the bartender leaned over to greet him; Bobo himself appeared. If you didn't know Father was a businessman you would have thought he was a celebrity. It wasn't only that he was good looking, people woke up when he was around. He didn't do anything special, his presence just made people feel good. Both Bobo and the captain escorted Father to the table. The fuss people made over Father was another reason I liked Bobo's.

Father explained that after dinner he was going on to the opening of a nightclub. The owners were clients. Otherwise he would have asked me along ("I think your mother wants you to keep an eye on me"). Father got the same treatment leaving as arriving. He had the car outside and drove me to the apartment. He told me not to wait up for him, which I had no intention of doing anyhow.

Our place was an eight-room duplex. You could see the water from almost every room. We had been there four years. The first time I saw it no one told me it was a duplex. I walked around the first floor. There seemed to be something wrong. I saw a kitchen, two big rooms, a smaller room, and a bathroom. Where were the bedrooms? Upstairs was where—three rooms and a storeroom, the only room you couldn't see the water from.

I loved the beach house, but the apartment was more comfortable. For one thing, there was endless hot water. My bathroom had a seven-foot bathtub and a bidet, which my friends got a kick out of, and a marble sink as big as a desk.

I thought of phoning Hillyer as a joke and asking him how he was making out—it was just the kind of thing he would have done—but instead I got into bed with the copy of Emily Dickinson Melissa had also given me. I saw a poem

I had never noticed, and before I went to sleep I decided to give the book to Zina and write the page of the poem as an inscription.

> Wild Nights —Wild Nights!
> Were I with thee
> Wild Nights should be
> Our luxury!
>
> Futile—the Winds—
> To a Heart in port—
> Done with a Compass —
> Done with a Chart!
>
> Rowing in Eden —
> Ah, the Sea!
> Might I but moor—Tonight —
> In Thee!

I woke at 2 A.M., I suppose because I had gone to bed early, and I got up to see if Father was home. His bedroom was empty, but a small light came from the first floor. I went downstairs on tiptoe. The guestroom door was closed. The light in the hall was the light from under the door. I could hear someone inside. I must have been half asleep, because for an instant I thought it was Hillyer and his girl, who for some reason couldn't stay at his apartment. Then of course I realized it was Father. I went upstairs and got back into bed. I didn't want to know any more about it. Was it Mrs. Mertz? Had she come into town? Had he made a date to meet her at the nightclub?

A few years earlier, when the facts of life were circulating around my classroom, I asked Father if what I heard was true. More or less, he said, and added that when two people make love they make something out of nothing. It was an act of pure creation. He didn't say anything about marriage.

I woke late the next morning and stayed in bed as long as I could. I wanted to make sure Father was gone. Silently I opened my door and listened before going into the hallway.

The apartment sounded empty. In my parents' room the bedclothes were turned back and one of the pillows was punched. Downstairs in the guestroom the pullout couch was closed. But I could smell cigarettes. The ashtray was empty but dirty, so I cleaned it. Father didn't smoke. I was covering up. On the table was a note: "Michael, if you want to ride out with me late this afternoon, call the office. On the other hand, Strangfeld is meeting the one o'clock train if you want to go out earlier. You didn't miss much last night. P." He always signed himself "P." I once told him I would have preferred "Father." He said, "P stands, not for Peter, but Pater—no, Pop."

Mr. Strangfeld picked me up at one. Zina had asked me to bring her a leaf from town—there were almost no trees on the Point. I got a big maple leaf at the station. On the way to the house I asked Mr. Strangfeld if he had driven anyone else in the day before. "*Nein, keiner,*" he said.

"*Danke,*" I said. "*Bitte,*" he said. So Mrs. Mertz and Zina had both been at the Point last night.

Mother was cheery. I told her about everything but the busy guestroom. She enjoyed the description of Father's elegant entrance at Bobo's and pretended to disapprove of Hillyer's assignation but really was amused. I asked how the lunch had gone with Mrs. Mertz.

"Good," was all she'd say. "I'm sure you'll hear about it from Zina," she added.

I changed into my bathing suit and took the maple leaf to the guesthouse. Mrs. Mertz was sunbathing in front, and Zina was reading on the deck, in back.

She sat up straight and held out her hand to kiss, like a courtly lady.

I gave her the leaf. "Why did you want this?"

"So you would return to me."

"Why wouldn't I return to you?"

"You might have forgotten me on your travels."

I looked at what she was reading. *The Waning of the Middle Ages*.

I ached to tell her about Father. It would have been a binding secret between us. But if Mrs. Mertz found out that Father had girlfriends it might encourage her.

As Zina twirled the leaf between her fingers she told me about lunch. "They were very femmy-chummy. They talked about the problems of being married to attractive men. They talked about running two households—we had a country place, too, when Father lived with us—and the problem of bringing up gifted, only children."

"Did Mother say I was gifted?"

"Definitely."

"Did she say what my gift was?"

"I'm your gift, Misha. I want you to kiss this leaf." She held it against her mouth. I closed my eyes and leaned forward. She removed the leaf, and I kissed her lips.

8

The Beach Party

MOTHER PROPOSED A joint beach party with the Mertzes.

She took it upon herself to invite Melissa for me and suggested the Mertzes invite whomever they wanted. I suspected Mother hoped they would invite men friends who would put me out of business with Zina and Father out of business with Mrs. Mertz, if there was any business. Melissa would be a problem. With her around I wouldn't be able to pay much attention to Zina. But then an idea occurred to me. I'd invite Ari Galaktos, a friend from school who was stuck in town for the summer. Ari was a poet and had actually published a poem. Melissa might go for him. Also, Ari was taller than Melissa.

The party was scheduled for Saturday night, three days off. In one afternoon Sonya, Blackheart, and I collected enough firewood for two beach parties. The ocean tides, sweeping by the Point, deposit all sorts of things on the beach. You wake up one morning and there are thousands of clam and oyster shells along the shoreline. Tires turn up, bottles, dead fish, dog carcasses, once a horse, cork and plastic floats, seaweed, tackle, jellyfish, and lots of wood—boards, planks, ties, beams, logs, crates, oars. Because wood floats and is carried at full tide to the high-water line it tends to stay on the beach, while jetsam can litter the shore one day and be gone the next.

We carried wood from as far as half a mile away and piled it on the beach in front of the house. Sonya supervised empty-mouthed, while Blackheart was practically lifting his own weight and carrying it stiff-necked like a soldier. Sonya would give him a bark when he dropped it devotedly in front of her. He mistook this and started leaping around her. She nipped him on the nose, and he scurried back to the house, I would say with his tail between his legs, but it was too short.

When we were done Zina came out with her camera and in the late afternoon sun posed me holding a series of bleached branches at my side. I was the hunter, this was my kill. I stood with my free hand shading my eyes; I stood smiling and looking proudly at the limb; I stood glancing apprehensively over my shoulder. The tips of one of the branches actually looked like antlers. Then she brought out a tripod and took a picture of me holding her by the hair, her arms dangling and her eyes closed. Later when I showed that one to Father he said, "You two should have exchanged roles."

Mr. Strangfeld delivered Ari Saturday morning. Ari, who was sixteen, had a long, dark face, heavy eyebrows, and a reserved manner. "He'll be a diplomat," Mother once said. "Or a butler," Father added.

An hour later Mr. Cuddihy dropped Melissa off on the bayside. Ari and I were there to meet her and carry her things across the Point. When I took her to her room she said, "I have something for you."

"No presents, Melissa."

"It's not a present, but it is for you." She handed me a folded piece of paper. "Read it by yourself."

I left her to change and took the paper to my room.

THOUGHTS FOR A BEACH PARTY

We're all alone—at least the others are
asleep. We touch and smile. No words, just thoughts,
of which a chance one sparkles, and we laugh.
There'll come a day, I fear, when you are out

of reach and memory is all of you
I have; and then another day when that
is gone. That morning I'll awake and rise
and eat an ordinary breakfast, dress
and go to leave—to find that I forgot
a certain necessary something, just
my comb, my keys, a paper, or a book—
a light makes darkness clearly black: a part
of me is lost. And then I'll wonder what
you were and where you were and try to reason
out an emptiness and hunt for non-
existent strings to pull you back in view.
What then? These words I've understood and truths
I've known because of you, these lonely fires
that add a little light and comfort on
the mind's black stretching beach of night,
the shifting tide forgetfulness will rise
and snuff them out, when it has carried you,
who lit them off to sea. What fumbling hand
and wet will kindle up the blazes then?

Walking downstairs with Melissa to lunch, I told her I
liked the poem, which was true, but that wasn't my main feeling. Mainly I was uncomfortable that she was writing poems
for me at all.

After lunch I motioned Ari to come to my room and asked him what he thought of Melissa. Ari was always polite. I might as well have asked him what he thought of lunch. I showed him the poem. He read it carefully.

"It's good," he said. "Take the first line, 'We're all alone—at least the others are.' It works two ways. The others are asleep, but they're alone too. And the line 'the mind's black stretching beach of night.' It's one foot short, so you have to say it slowly, you have to *stretch* it out." He saw other things I hadn't seen. Then he asked me if I was going with Melissa.

"She's all yours," I said.

The plan was to have drinks on the bayside porch at seven and move to the ocean beach at eight. Zina and Mrs. Mertz brought one guest, a man about fifty named Max Pondoro. He was the only one dressed up—white slacks, brown and white shoes, paisley shirt, and navy blazer. Mrs. Mertz herself had caught the spirit of the thing—she came barefoot, in jeans and a man's frayed shirt. Zina was proper in bell-bottom slacks and a pale blue blouse.

Max Pondoro kissed Mother's hand and said how kind she was to have invited him. He kissed Melissa's hand and said what a pretty young lady she was. He bowed slightly as he shook Father's hand, which brought out Father's big smile. Only Ari was up to Mr. Pondoro—he bowed back.

I left the porch at seven-thirty to start the fire. Zina came with me. "My mother is a genius," she said. "Did you see Max's way with your mother?"

"No." I had, of course.

"Well, watch at the party. Mother told him to play up to her."

"Why did she do that?"

"To make her feel attractive. You have to admit, Max was made for the job."

"My mother feels perfectly attractive. She *is* perfectly attractive. She doesn't need some dummy kissing her hand."

"Misha! My mother is trying to be nice. She felt your mother was upset and needed a little perking up. That's all."

"She *was* upset, and it's over."

"Misha, you're mad at us. We love you, and we love your mother. Come here!" She pulled me to her, put her arms around me, and hugged me. Then she held me away and said, "All right?"

"All right," I said. I knew she was doing to me what Max Pondoro was doing to Mother. But it *was* all right. Zina's body was soft and hard, and I could smell the scent of her soap.

When we got the fire started I pulled out a tarred board that was smoking. Otherwise the fire was fine, big enough to be fun, but not so hot you couldn't cook over it. Besides franks, hamburgers, and marshmallows, there was wine and beer. Mrs. Mertz brought a thermos of martinis, and Father a bottle of scotch. The air was cool and dry, and there were no bugs. We sang rounds, "Frère Jacques," "Dona Nobis Pacem." Everyone slipped food to the dogs, and Blackheart spit up. Father, Zina, and I were on one blanket; Ari and Melissa on another; Mrs. Mertz, squatting, poked the fire with a stick and sipped a martini. And, sure enough, there was Max Pondoro chatting Mother up. She was laughing. Well, why not?

By firelight Zina took on a new kind of beauty. Her dark, tanned face had red in it, and her brown eyes were shiny black. She told a ghost story about a witch who was deserted by her lover for another woman. The witch turned herself into a pig and mingled with the man's other pigs. She was the most succulent pig of all, and when Christmas came the man chose her for Christmas dinner. But just before the slaughter she ate the leaves of a deadly henbane bush grow-ing at the edge of the wood, and when the couple ate her flesh they died a fearful death.

"Is the moral," Father said, "not to eat pig or not to lie down with witches?"

"I think," Mother said, "it's watch out for any woman who makes a pig of herself."

87

"I think the moral of the story," Melissa said, "is that love is worth dying for."

"It's your story," Father said to Zina. "What's the moral?"

"Melissa has the right answer."

The fire turned to embers. Father suggested we walk along the beach. Mother had fallen asleep. Max Pondoro and Mrs. Mertz said they would stay and guard her. The water was black except for the phosphorescent lights in the hollows of the waves. Backlit clouds passed in front of the moon. Melissa, walking behind us with Ari, recited Matthew Arnold's "Dover Beach."

> The sea is calm to-night.
> The tide is full, the moon lies fair
> Upon the straits. . . .
> Ah, love, let us be true
> To one another! for the world, which seems
> To lie before us like a land of dreams,
> So various, so beautiful, so new,
> Hath neither joy, nor love, nor light,
> Nor certitude, nor peace, nor help for pain. . . .

The poem was beautiful, but it was wrong about the world. The world at the moment was Zina and Father and I walking on this perfect beach on this perfect night. Mother content. Mrs. Mertz probably staring into the embers. Melissa and Ari discovering each other.

Father felt it. "How dear we are to one another!" he said.

Zina felt it too. "Without one another we might as well die. Isn't that what the poem means, Melissa?"

"Yes."

When we got back to the fire only Mr. Pondoro was there. Mrs. Mertz had gone to bed. It seems that when Mother woke she wanted to know where everyone was. Mr. Pondoro tried to tell her, but she didn't believe him. She said she was going to the guesthouse to look for herself, and that was the last he saw of her.

That pretty much ended the party. But the night wasn't over. I woke, at what time I don't know. The moon was gone, the room was dark. Blackheart had his paws on my chest and was whining. Someone else was in bed beside me. At first it seemed to be Mother, who for some reason thought I was still a baby. Then it was Zina, who now understood how much I loved her. But it was Melissa. "Is it all right to be here?" she whispered. She put her arm around me, and we kissed. The trouble was, when I had awakened I was having a sex dream. I could no more have turned away from Melissa than I could have stopped the dream. She smelled so sweet.

We didn't do anything besides kiss, but it happened to me. I held her, and we kissed some more. Then I fell asleep. When I woke in the morning she was gone.

After lunch Father and I sailed Melissa, Ari, and Mr. Pondoro across the bay to town. On the dock Melissa squeezed my hand and whispered, "Write me your thoughts." Ari embraced me and whispered, "Thanks." What did he think he was thanking me for?

When we got back to the Point I wanted to go right away to the guesthouse, but I held off till later in the afternoon.

Zina was alone on the deck.

"Misha, I want to tell you something about yourself. You are actually older right now than you will be in a few years. You'll be younger then and enjoy yourself more. For instance, why did you let Ari scoop Melissa up like that?"

"He didn't scoop her up."

"Misha, I was there. I saw it. And you didn't raise a finger."

"Melissa came into my room last night. She came into my bed."

"Is that true?"

"Yes."

"Well, Misha," she said with a sly smile, "I hope you were a gentleman."

"I was *not* a gentleman."

"You don't understand me. I hope you didn't send her away. That would have been very ungentlemanly indeed."

She was so pleased with herself. I could have struck her. I called to Blackheart and stalked off toward the house. He ran beside me, barking and jumping.

9

On Love

THE NEXT AFTERNOON Mr. Strangfeld dropped Hillyer off. Hillyer was big, with kind of a small head. He was over six feet and weighed a hundred and ninety, most of it muscle, which was a mystery because he didn't move around much. Mother loved to watch him eat. That night she roasted two chickens, and he ate one by himself. Also, Father liked to play straight man to Hillyer. I think it was with this in mind that he asked him if the boys at school worried about venereal disease.

"We pretty much stick to virgins, sir."

Father asked what happened after they ceased to be virgins.

"We move on, sir."

"Is there an inexhaustible supply?"

"If you know where to look."

"Where is that?"

"Among younger girls, sir. You can always find one among younger girls."

"There must be a limit even there."

"As we go down the age scale some of us lose interest, so demand never exceeds supply, if you see what I mean, sir."

Although the next morning was clear, a strong wind from the ocean lifted sand along the beach. Instead of swimming we took the Angela out on the bay. When the wind comes off the ocean, chopping it up, it blows into the bay and keeps the water tight. Four of us were just the right weight for the Angela—she really dug in. Hillyer was a good sailor, and we all took turns at the tiller, even Mother.

After lunch Hillyer, Blackheart, and I went for a walk to the end of the Point. The only thing we passed was the wreck of the Rita M, which ran aground in the great storm of 1938. The hull had lain exposed on the beach until World War II, when the Army Engineers, to stop erosion, constructed a two-thousand-foot stone jetty from the tip of the Point into the sea. As a result the tides collected sand in the pocket. The bay beach built up, and the wreck was mostly buried.

All you could see now was the bleached fo'c's'le sticking up sideways.

We sat down beside it, Blackheart sniffed it and peed on it, and Hillyer broke out some pot. Pot is special on a bare beach in bright sunlight. There's not much to fasten your eyes on. Waves and clouds become important. Hillyer and I chose favorite clouds and argued their merits as they passed overhead.

Hillyer's girl, it turned out, was named Rita. He said that at first he thought I was kidding with the story of the Rita M, but then he realized I didn't know his girl's name. He thought the coincidence was fantastic, especially after a few more puffs. He said that Rita's nipples were like the dials of a safe. The current combination was two turns to the left on the right one and three turns to the right on the left one. "But the combination keeps changing. You have to experiment."

I asked him if he was in love with Rita.

He said he didn't believe in love, and if you don't believe in it you can't be in it. "It's like mortal sin. If you don't believe in it, you can't commit it." Hillyer was a Catholic.

I pointed out that that logic didn't work for, say, diseases. "I'll give you a test," I went on. "If you had to choose between saving your mother from a sinking ship and saving Rita, which would you save?"

"My mother's a pain in the ass."

"Your father then."

"Pain in the ass."

"Is there anyone you'd save instead of Rita?"

"Hannah."

"Who's Hannah?"

"Ben Fogarty's sister." Ben was in our class.

"Why would you save her?"

"Did you ever see her? You'd save her if you saw her."

"Are you in love with Hannah?"

"I don't *believe* in love."

"What do you mean, you don't believe in love? Do you think when people say they're in love they don't feel the things they think they feel?"

"Wha?"

"You're just being dumb."

"So what is love?"

"It's more than wanting to screw someone. It's wanting to be with them, listen to them, think about them. You treasure everything about them, a shoe, a handkerchief."

"Snot."

"What's not?"

"Snot, snot," he said and wiped his nose with the back of his hand.

"Oh, come on!"

"So what's love good for?"

"People in love are exalted."

He took a puff.

I took a puff and decided to tell him about Zina. As soon as he heard the name he chanted, "Zin-*a*! Hann-*ah*! Rit-*a*!" and we broke up. We staggered into the water to cool off. Hillyer fell down, and we broke up again.

A trip to the end of the Point included a walk on the Rocks. The Rocks were the jetty the Army Engineers built with blocks of trap rock dynamited from cliffs on the mainland. The blocks were as much as seven feet across. You could see drill marks where charges had been set to sever them. The Engineers got the blocks in place on a small-gauge railroad they constructed on a trestle beside the jetty site. You could still see railroad pilings sticking out of the water. After a rough tide or heavy rain the algae on the Rocks swelled with water and made them slippery. You were always hearing how a fisherman from the mainland had lost his footing and drowned. The only way to walk the Rocks, wet or dry, was the way we were walking, barefoot. Strong prehensile toes helped. This day the Rocks were hot and dry. The algae lay flat and sticky and actually gave us an extra purchase.

But even dry the Rocks could be dangerous. There was a section near the end called Three Rock Edge, where the blocks had been awkwardly fitted. They presented edges up rather than horizontal planes. To get over, you had to straddle the edges and walk spread-eagle. My first time on Three Rock Edge, Father went before me, walking backwards to show me how to do it. Instead of walking, I sat on the edge, legs on either side, and inched across. I thought Father would be disappointed with me, but he squeezed my shoulder. On the way back I walked it upright. I was eight that summer.

Now when we reached Three Rock Edge I couldn't coax Hillyer across. It occurred to me that for some reason Hillyer's caution was connected with his denial of love. It also occurred to me that he didn't have a father like mine. Blackheart never tried to get across Three Rock Edge. He would take up a position on the last flat rock and whine until I came back. Today he was pleased to have another coward for company.

At supper Hillyer asked Father if he believed in love and then included Mother, "Ma'am?"

"Romantic love?" Father said.

"Yes, sir."

"Why do you ask?"

I think Father thought this was the beginning of one of Hillyer's routines.

"Because Michael does, and I don't."

"Are you asking if I believe in its existence or if I recommend it?"

"Both, sir."

"Many people claim to have experienced it."

"Have you, sir?"

"Hillyer, my good wife is here beside me. If I had never felt it could I say so? On the other hand, if I had felt it often could I say that? But the answer is yes, of course."

Father looked disappointed that nothing developed from the exchange. Apparently Hillyer really wanted to know what Father thought.

After the meal Father picked up a book and lay down on a couch. Hillyer said he would do the dishes. Mother said he could only dry. I wandered with Blackheart down to the water's edge. I always checked the ocean in the evening. Tonight it was unusually still. Small waves broke quietly on the shore. On windless evenings in summer I thought the ocean was false. How could something so big and heavy in the body be so dainty in the fingertips?

I didn't hear Zina approach and started at the touch of her hand on my shoulder. Her face was blue and pink in the dusk. For a second I could have kissed her. I don't know why I didn't. It would have been the perfect act of love. She bent down, picked up a shell, and scaled it, hollow side up. It skipped twice in the water, floated for an instant, and sank. I scaled a shell, hollow down; it captured air, hovered, tipped, and slipped into the water. Gulls circled overhead, thinking there was something for them. Zina took my hand like a child's, looked down at it, and said, "You've been avoiding me. You're angry with me."

I said I wasn't.

"Let me try to explain something to you, Misha. I know you don't like me talking about Melissa, but I want to say that at first I was sorry for Melissa. But when you told me what happened the night of the party I decided that she can take care of herself. It's you I should have been concerned about. I'm not saying you should be grateful to Melissa, I'm saying don't burn your bridges. Give yourself a chance, give Melissa a chance. You may not think so now, but—listen to me! don't look away!—you may want to do again what you did that night. Don't burn your bridges, is all I'm saying. Is that something to get upset about?"

"But I don't *want* to do it again."

"Maybe not now."

"Now or ever. You're trying to get rid of me."

"*No*, Misha! All right, not another word. But don't be angry with me. I'm only trying to help you. Say you're not angry."

I had lost my breath. "Come up to the house and meet my friend from school," was all I could say.

As we walked barefoot through the soft sand she took my hand again and said, "Things are running through you very fast. Be careful!"

How do I do that, I thought.

Everyone was on the bayside porch. "You found him," Mother said.

Mrs. Mertz was there. As she drew on her cigarette, her eyes glistened. She looked like a vampire. "As for me," she was saying, "I adore it, every part of it, even the heartbreak. Being in love is like driving up the California coast. It gives you the illusion that life will work out."

"How about when it's over?" Mother said.

"The secret is, do it again, instantly."

"You're saying you can fall in love at will."

"If you are predisposed, if you are in the *mode*, if you are looking for love—love will find you."

"It sounds like being in heat," Mother said. "How can you do it at will? It does take someone else, or does it?"

"Of course." Mrs. Mertz paused to sip her drink. "Let me say that I believe one is born with the capacity or not."

"I still don't understand why it's so prized. Is it good to be vulnerable?"

"Is it good to take a chance? If we don't take a chance we don't have a chance. Love, like butter, makes things better."

Out of the corner, where he was sitting in a deep chair, Hillyer said to Father, "You never said, sir, whether you recommend love."

"I recommend it to mankind, Hillyer, but not to each and

every member thereof. Love and its works were intended as a consolation for the human condition. I expect there were times when it wouldn't have taken much for us to give up the human enterprise. We need all the rewards we can get. What do you think?" he said to Zina.

"It seems to me my mother is describing something pleasant, but it doesn't sound like love."

"Ah!" Mother said with satisfaction.

"You're speaking from experience?" Father asked.

Zina said nothing.

"Are you?" Father said.

"Maybe Zina doesn't want to tell you," Mother said. "As for me, I don't think love is a consolation for the human condition, I think it's part of the human condition. Sometimes it works out, and sometimes it doesn't, like most things in life. But it's always a delusion. The beloved does not live up to expectations, and when love persists beyond disappointment it becomes a snare as well."

I said, "Why doesn't the beloved live up to expectations?"

"Because the expectations are high and the beloved is flawed." She turned to Father and said, "Tell him!"

When Father was silent she said again, "*Tell* him!"

"I agree," was all he would say.

Everyone fell silent, and after a bit Mother said, "Let's go in, away from the mosquitoes."

There were no mosquitoes. Mrs. Mertz and Zina excused themselves and went back to the guesthouse. The rest of us settled down inside. Mother fixed drinks for Father and herself.

"Hillyer," Mother said, "if you want to talk more about love, go ahead."

"No, ma'am, you and Mrs. Mertz explained it all."

That amused Mother and closed the subject. We played Scrabble, and later, going up the stairs, Hillyer said he would save Zina even before Hannah. "Zin-*a*! Zin-*a*! Zin-*a*!" he chanted.

10

Led Astray

I WOKE LATE the next morning. Mother and Hillyer were having breakfast. They stopped talking when I came into the kitchen. I asked where Father was. Mr. Strangfeld had picked him up, along with Zina and Mrs. Mertz. I was put off that Zina hadn't told me her plans.

I asked Mother why Zina and Mrs. Mertz had gone to town.

She said she didn't know.

I asked when they would be back.

"Michael, I don't *know*."

"When is Father coming back?"

"Tomorrow."

"Did Father have to go to the office?"

"Michael, you can ask everyone these questions when they get back. I'm not a social secretary."

Suddenly Hillyer suggested I return to town with him and stay over at his place. I expected Mother to veto that, but she said to go ahead. Later when Hillyer and I were alone I asked him what he and Mother had been talking about.

"You."

"I knew it. What about?"

"She wanted to know what was up with you and Zina."

"She thinks something's up?"

"She thinks you're in for trouble."

"What else?"

"She asked me to invite you to town."

"She thinks you'll lead me astray and save me from Zina."

"That's our plan."

"My own mother." I was amused, sort of.

We got to Hillyer's house about six. I was always struck by the size of his living room, with all the windows and the high ceiling. The bottoms of the windows were clear, and the tops were stained glass. When the sun hit them in the morning the room looked like a kaleidoscope.

Hillyer phoned for pizza, "with everything."

"No anchovies," I shouted.

"No anchovies," he said.

Then he phoned Rita. His plan was for her to come over later with a friend for me. After the pizzas I looked up "Mertz" in the phonebook. The address was ten minutes away. I phoned—the line was busy.

"Listen," I said, "I'm just going to walk over there and say hello. I'll be back."

Zina's place was a converted carriage house on a street along the water with lots of trees, more Zina's style than Mrs. Mertz's. A man in a tweed jacket, with watery blue eyes, answered the door.

I introduced myself. "I'm a friend of Zina's."

"Me too. Come on in. She's out. Mrs. M's fixing her face. I'm Jack Packard."

"Misha, what a surprise! How absolutely deliciously lovely to see you!" Mrs. Mertz in a red kimono stood in the doorway of the living room. "This is Mr. Packard. Misha lives next to us at the beach. I just put on some lipstick or I'd give you a big kiss. So you come over here and peck my cheek. Jack, fix drinks! And don't be fooled by Misha's youthful appearance. What's your drink, Misha? Vodka? Neat, and neat for me. It's been one thing after another. Just now Zina's father called from Europe. What a thrill to hang up on an international call! Zina's out. I know you didn't come to see this old flesh."

"I came to see you both, Mrs. Mertz."

"How gallant! Well, you'll have to do with me. Jack and I are going to dinner. We'll have all evening to talk. So you come in and entertain me while I change. And, Jack, after you deliver the drinks you stay out here. Misha and I have matters to discuss. Come along!"

The bedroom was more Mrs. Mertz's style—a dressing table with a mirrored top and flowered skirt, a high-backed upholstered chair, which she pointed me into, an unmade bed with pink sheets, and the smell of perfume and cosmetics.

She went into the bathroom, left the door ajar, and talked from there. "Why didn't you drive in with us this morning?"

"I didn't know you were coming in. Is Zina going with you to dinner?"

"No. Are you having dinner with your father?"

"No. I don't know what Father is doing. Are you and Zina coming back tomorrow?"

"I am. I don't know about Zina. Your father's picking me up at noon. Does he come to town to work?"

"Mostly. Is Zina having dinner with anyone?"

"Twenty-year-old girls tell their mothers as little as possible. Did your mother come in with you?"

"No. Zina told me she was twenty-one."

"She will be. Your mother must hate being alone out there."

"She doesn't mind if it's not too often. Did Zina come in because she didn't want to be alone?"

"Your father said he was an insurance broker. I'm not sure what that is."

"He finds the right carrier for clients and the right clients for carriers. He's not a salesman, he's an insurance expert. He has his own business." That's the way it went. She wanted to talk about my father, and I wanted to talk about her daughter. "Are these Zina's pictures on the wall?"

Each photograph—there were ten of them, black-and-white—had a vase in the foreground in sharp focus and part of a female nude in the background out of focus. The point was playing the lines and planes off one another.

"Yes, they're Zina's," Mrs. Mertz said and poked her head in the bathroom doorway. "Do you recognize the body?"

"Zina?"

"No, darling. Moi. I hope you're blushing." She withdrew.

I was blushing. Not because the pictures were of Mrs. Mertz, but because I had thought they were of Zina.

Mr. Packard came in with our drinks, gave me mine, and blindly reached Mrs. Mertz's into the bathroom.

"You can look, Jack. Misha is out there, looking more or less at the same thing."

Mrs. Mertz came out, still in the kimono, nothing changed except she was barefoot. She took a small black dress from the closet and said, "Cover your eyes!" In a minute she said, "Look!" The dress was shiny and tight. There was nothing to it. Otherwise she wore pearls and black high-heeled shoes. She posed for me, hands on hips, turning this way and that, but watching me. "What's the verdict?"

"Innocent."

"Not likely. Misha, let me see if I can tell what you're thinking. You're thinking Zina in jeans looks better. Right?"

I nodded. Why not, she was right.

"You're thinking . . . you're wondering if a time will ever come when you will really like a woman dressed like this."

She was exactly right.

"What else? You'll have to tell me, I can't guess any more. You don't have to be insulting, but there *is* something else."

"The hundred times I've seen my mother go out in the evening she never looked as good as you do now, is what I'm thinking."

"You *are* a charmer."

"It's true."

"Yes, but you're also thinking that nonetheless you prefer the way your mother looks. Don't say anything! It's too complicated. Come downstairs with us, we'll drop you off wherever you're going."

Back at Hillyer's Melissa opened the door.

It seems she had tried to get me at the Point, and Mother told her where I was. Melissa then called Hillyer and invited herself over. Hillyer called Rita and told her to cancel the friend.

Hillyer was dancing with Rita in the living room. I was surprised at how slight she was. She waved at me and said hi, and they went on dancing.

Melissa and I began to dance. I couldn't help thinking how much better Rita, small, would fit with me, and Melissa, big, with Hillyer. We must have looked like comedy couples. Melissa smelled good, the way she had after the party. We danced out of the living room, down to the end of the hall, and into a bedroom. I didn't even know whose it was. We closed the door and lay down on the bed. We did it twice. In between, Melissa told me her father had a drinking problem. He didn't sleep well, and he had veins in his nose. She said she had gone to the movies with Ari and asked if I minded. I didn't care, but I said it was okay as long as nothing happened. She said it hadn't and it wouldn't. I felt like telling her to go ahead and enjoy herself, the way Zina had told *me*, but it would have been impolite.

Melissa had soft, smooth skin and didn't seem so big lying beside me. She sang Beatles songs to me in her pretty voice, and I felt a genuine kind of affection for her. I couldn't understand why I wasn't upset. Even if the pact I had with Zina was only in my head, hadn't I broken it? Then I realized I had done exactly what Zina said I should do. I was obeying her.

I lay on my stomach, facing away. Melissa's head was pressed against my shoulder, her arm across my back. I tried to imagine she was Zina, but it didn't work. Melissa was quiet and content. I think Zina would have been walking up and down, talking. Then I tried to imagine Zina where she really was at that moment. I saw her sitting at a table. I couldn't see whom she was with—it was like a dream that tells you only certain things—but I could see her brown eyes and carved lips. I tried to hear what she was saying, but all that came through were things that she had already said to me. Then I fell asleep. Melissa woke me. She had to leave. I was pleased that I didn't resent her. I even felt a sense of responsibility for her. Again I was obeying Zina.

There was no sign of Rita and Hillyer. I left the outside door ajar, and we walked to Melissa's place. We went out of our way so we could walk along the water. The night was clear and dry, and the temperature absolutely perfect. You would be comfortable clothed or naked. The moon was thin and bright. We walked arm in arm, and every now and then Melissa pressed her breast against my arm.

"You know," she said, "I don't mind if you don't love me."

I said nothing.

"I care, but I don't mind."

"Do you have to love someone to go to bed with them?"

"I do, but you don't. Is that all right, Michael?"

"Would it be better if the other person was in love?"

"Of course."

"What's the difference if they love you back or not?"

"If they love you back they won't go away."

11

Protect Me

NEXT MORNING HILLYER was heating water in the kitchen and scratching his stomach with both hands.

"You two sure disappeared," he said. "Rita was shocked."

"I liked her."

"How do you know? It was hello and good night. How did it go?"

"It was okay."

"As good as that," he said, then deepening his voice, "We, on the other hand, did outrageously well."

"When Melissa and I left were you here?"

"I heard you go. In fact, I was in situ at the very moment. . . . There's no food in this house."

We agreed to have breakfast at my place. "But I have to call first. My father might be there."

"Your father is the best."

Hillyer felt so rotten about his parents breaking up I thought I'd let him know that things weren't necessarily perfect everywhere else. "Actually," I said, "I have to call because he might be in situ himself."

"I didn't know he situed around."

"Yep."

"Well, at least he still situes at home. You seem pretty blasé about it."

"He told me that people feel love is magical because it's making something out of nothing. If he wants to make something out of nothing, I can't get too excited about it. Also, it's his business."

"Absolutely. As long as no one finds out. If they do—and I mean your old lady—he'll make nothing out of something."

"Is that what your father did?"

"Yep."

I phoned home. Father was still there, about to leave for his office. He hadn't known I was in town. "You *must* tell me when you're coming to town," he said. Then in a lighter tone, "We might have had dinner."

"I couldn't. I was in situ."

"In what?" Then he got the joke. "Anyone I know?"

"A gentleman never tells."

"Quite right."

I asked about his plans for getting to the Point. He suggested he pick me up outside the apartment.

Father pulled up promptly, with Mrs. Mertz beside him. Zina was in the back. I got in beside her. She took my hand and squeezed it. Father gave me his big smile in the rearview mirror, and Mrs. Mertz continued talking. It was a while before I realized she was talking about a recent trip to Russia.

"The people of course suffer. Italians eat, the French talk, the Germans make, and Russians suffer. It's their métier, and now they have no culture to protect them from the suffering. No cuisine. No etiquette. Everyone wants to leave. You should see the hard-currency whores in the tourist hotels. And very attractive whores they are. You look at them, and you say to yourself the Russians have put the flower of their womanhood into prostitution."

"I came to see you at your place last night," I whispered to Zina.

"Mother told me."

I waited for Zina to say where she had been, but she didn't.

"I asked one of the girls," Mrs. Mertz went on, "what her favorite nationality was. 'The Japs,' she said, 'they pay well and they're quick.'"

Mrs. Mertz thought Father was enjoying this, but I could tell from his polite nods that he wasn't. As for me, I had not expected to be driving back with Zina, and I was pleased. Every now and then she touched my hand.

We pulled into the station parking lot. Mr. Strangfeld was waiting with his beach buggy. Father got in front, and Mrs. Mertz squeezed in back with Zina and me. She kept talking. Everyone stopped listening but Mr. Strangfeld, who said *"Ja!"* a couple of times.

Finally Mrs. Mertz said something to him in German, which tickled him, and he said, *"Ja, ja, ja!"*

We got off on the hard sand, and as we trudged up to the house through the soft sand Blackheart barked behind the screen door. Mother was there watching us. She let Blackheart out but didn't come out herself. Mrs. Mertz gave Father a parting kiss on the cheek, a mistake. When we got inside, Mother was gone. Father and I changed and went for a swim. The ocean was in a late afternoon mood, smooth and cool. We avoided talking about town, I thought.

Mother brought it up at supper. "Did you get done everything you wanted to get done?" she said to Father.

"Just about."

"Did Mrs. Mertz get done everything she wanted to get done?"

Father gave her his ironical quizzical look.

"I asked you a question."

"I don't know the answer."

I said, "I went to the Mertzes' last evening, and Mrs. Mertz was going out to dinner with a man named Jack Packard."

"Would you say she got done what she wanted to get done?" Father said to me.

"I'd say she probably did. Zina wasn't there."

Mother stared down at her plate for a few seconds. We said nothing. She burst into tears. Father indicated that I should leave them alone. I went to my room.

Whatever Father was up to, I don't remember blaming him very much. I suppose I didn't take the problems between him and Mother seriously. And, sure enough, the next morning she was sunny, even though it was raining. Father had soothed her. Blackheart lay on his stomach by the stove, watching carefully, ready for fun. Mother asked me what I wanted for breakfast.

Zina appeared at the kitchen door. "Can Misha come out and play?"

"Sure," I said.

"Zina asked me," Mother said, "and you haven't had your breakfast. Come in, dear. Have you had breakfast?"

"There's a lovely warm rain out here that I don't want to miss."

I picked up a piece of coffee cake and gave Mother a mock-imploring look.

"Go!" she said. She really was in a good mood. Blackheart jumped to his feet.

My first recollection of warm rain was when I was five and Father carried me from the boat we had then up the bay beach and over the Point to the house. Out on the bay the rain had started gradually, and the sky turned yellow, the way it was now. We were tacking to shore in a slow wind, and I got grazed by the boom. It was nothing. Nonetheless Father beached the boat and carried me home like a baby. I remember looking up at the yellow sky and liking the warm rain.

Now Zina and I walked along the water's edge. The ocean too had a yellow tinge. Zina wore a white cotton blouse, which soon was wet and clung to her breasts. I didn't look at them directly, but I could see them. They were small in depth and large around. I suppose it would have been arousing if it had been any other girl, but I didn't think of Zina that way. What I felt included sex, but the whole thing was so much more important than sex.

The water was pocked and subdued by falling rain. We shared the coffee cake. She sucked the crumbs off her fingers and then off mine. I told her about Father carrying me in the rain, and, the most remarkable thing, she told me that her first recollection of warm rain was walking hand in hand with her father at low tide on the beach of the French resort Ile de Ré.

"Was the sky yellow?"

"I think so. What I remember most was feeling safe. We walked far out in the water. It seemed never to get deep. My father said the tide came in very fast and we had to be careful. He said it, I think, to give me a thrill, but he couldn't scare me, I felt so safe. You've never been to Europe."

"Not besides being born there."

"How I'd like to show it to you! The first time Americans see Europe is like the first time they make love. They never forget it. Americans think they invented everything. But it all comes from Europe, the buildings, the furniture, the language. We'd spend a week in London and go to the theater every night. Then a week in Paris. Then we'd take the Paris-Rome overnight and stay up to see the Alps by moonlight."

"Could we really go? If I went to Father and said we wanted to go to Europe and he said yes, would you really go?"

"Wouldn't that be splendid! And it would help me."

"How do you mean?"

"Misha, I want you to protect me."

"How do you mean?"

"I'm in danger."

"What kind of danger?"

"I want you to protect me."

"Of course I'll protect you. I love you."

"I know you do, that's why I can ask you."

"How are you in danger?"

"You know I'm a very self-controlled person."

"Yes," I said, although I didn't particularly.

"I'm losing control."

"Of what?"

"Of myself."

"In what way?"

"Misha, I just want you to protect me." She put her hand over my mouth, put her face close to mine, withdrew her hand like the leaf, and kissed me on the lips.

What was I supposed to do? The only sense I could make of it was that she was having some kind of mental trouble.

That evening—the rain had stopped—I invited Father to check out the ocean and told him about Zina. I thought maybe he should speak to Mrs. Mertz and suggest a doctor. He said it didn't have to be mental trouble, it could be anything.

"Maybe you should talk to her yourself," I said. "Maybe she'd tell *you* what it was, and we could help her."

He said he might, and I felt better. But that night I had a dream. I was standing on a station platform in a foreign country. Zina was in a train that was pulling out and was trying to tell me something through the window. But I couldn't hear her. I tried to get on the train, but it was going too fast. When I woke I knew what it was. She had fallen in love.

After breakfast I got Father alone again and told him my dream and what I thought it meant. He nodded but didn't really say anything.

In mid-morning Zina came by with Sonya and asked if Blackheart could go for a walk. I called him, and off he went, looking back to see if I was coming. As soon as they were out of sight I went to the guesthouse. Mrs. Mertz was sunning herself on the deck. "Hello, darling Misha. Zina went for a walk."

"I came to see you, Mrs. Mertz."

"People are beginning to talk, Misha."

The only way to get into the subject was to tell her right off what Zina had said and ask her what she made of it. She sat up and listened carefully.

"I don't know what to tell you, Misha, except that Zina is a high-strung girl. Not to go into details, she has had her share of problems, as who has not. Just what this one is, I don't know. But let me put it another way. Both Zina and I tend toward the dramatic. I suspect whatever it is it's not life threatening."

"Do you think she's fallen in love with someone?"

She gave me a shrewd look. "Those things are so . . . transitory. I don't take them seriously until the people move in together."

"Has Zina been in love before?"

"Every young girl has been in love before."

"Then she has."

"There was the boy with the Chinese eyes. There was . . . But, Misha, ask her yourself. She'll tell you."

"Would Henry know?"

"He's a terrible gossip. He probably would. I must have the boys down. They *are* diverting. Henry took an especial shine to you. Well, ring him up, darling. He'll take you to the best restaurant in town. His gallery is the St. Sébastien, not very original."

12

A Friend of Love

FRIDAY I TOOK Mrs. Mertz and Hillyer to town in the Angela.

"I know what Misha is up to, Hillyer," Mrs. Mertz said, "but what about you?"

"I'm just relaxing. How about you, ma'am?"

"I'm up to no good."

"Sounds good."

"Let's hope so."

We moored in the marina. Mrs. Mertz and Hillyer went their way, and I went to the Galerie St. Sébastien. It was on the second floor of the town's only art deco building. A pretty woman at a desk asked if she could help me. When I told her why I was there she gave me a wonderful smile, said that Henry was busy with a client, wouldn't be long, would I like to look at the show in the meantime? She handed me the catalogue.

Without it I would have thought the paintings were by a child. Stick figures in bright colors. A house with a door, two windows, chimney, smoke. A mailman and a dog, a red wagon, a cat with whiskers.

A bearded man was standing back and looking with amusement at the paintings. He asked me if I liked them. I said I did, but I thought I could have done them myself.

"Precisely why you like them," he said.

He was about to begin a conversation when Henry came up behind me, locked my elbows in his hands, and whispered into my ear, "These little items start at fifteen big ones."

"Hundreds?"

"Thousands. Like them?"

I said the same thing, I liked them, but I could have done them myself.

"Not so. You think you could have, but you missed your chance. At four or five, but not now. The thing about Odo, Odo Fürst, is there's a part of him that's still five years old. This is Odo's first—oops, pun—his first show, and it's a grand success. They came all the way from New York to review it, and you and I are going to celebrate at the best restaurant in town."

The pretty woman reminded Henry that he had an appointment at three. He told her to put it off till the next day.

The restaurant, along the water, was Les Deux Amis, which I had heard about but not been to. It was run by a young couple, who told Henry they were coming to see his new show "soonest."

Henry struck me as very handsome, with his deep tan and large, bright eyes. He told me he had been born in the Midwest, studied art history at Yale, "done advertising" in New York, and came here twelve years ago with a friend. The friend had sold him his half of the gallery, and here he still was. "Now how about you? Zina says you're a real American."

"I don't know what that means."

"Well, if I saw you on the street, hadn't heard your voice, and your clothes didn't give you away, I'd say you were . . . Milanese. I'd also say that your parents adore you, that your father is a judge, very proud of your academic record. He thinks you'll be a scholar. Your mother knows your lighter side because she's seen you among your contemporaries. She knows you're destined to be loved, even though you will always present a somber face to the world."

"My mother thinks I'm in for trouble."

"Why, for heaven's sake?"

"She thinks I'm heading for a fall."

"Does she think you're expecting too much from life?"

"Something like that."

"You want to be a genius."

"No, she thinks that about Zina. I don't want to be a genius, I want to be happy."

"Then definitely don't be a genius. Zina is not a genius, by the way. She has talent and will do fine if she works hard. Photography doesn't have many geniuses. It's too easy to be good and too hard to be better than good. Tell your mother that Zina is not a genius. And tell her—no, better not— there's something you could be right now. I know twenty photographers at least who are *searching* for you. There's a lovely intensity about you, Misha. The agencies would just gobble you up. That is, if you never smiled. What you'd be selling is severity. After a year of it your face would be famous. Then one day a photographer catches you off guard. 'Say *formaggio*,' he says, and you smile. The spell is broken. Your career is over."

He went on like this, describing my marriage to and divorce from "a very rich, older, I mean older, woman." With money from the settlement I move to Switzerland and become "the toast of Zurich," but my destiny lies in North Africa. . . .

This was making me uncomfortable, and he stopped. He ordered sole Véronique for us. I had never had fish with fruit before. It was the best thing I had ever tasted.

The more he talked, the more I thought it was Henry that Zina was in love with. I also thought he was being so nice because he was happy about it. I asked him how long he had known Zina.

"Years and years. I lured them up here. So, tell me, what are you studying in school?"

"The regular things. Do you know Zina's father?"

"Self-important. We can't figure how Mrs. M stood him so long."

"Does Zina show her pictures at your gallery?"

"All we do is painting and a little sculpture. Those photos you took of Zina are quite remarkable. Does photography interest you?"

"Not really, but I like Zina's pictures. Did you see the beach grass?"

"And your *feet*. You'll have poems written to those feet before you're done."

And that's the way it went. Finally I said, "Henry, may I ask you something personal? You don't have to answer if you don't want to. Are you and Zina going together?"

He was taken aback, at first I thought because I had discovered his secret. Then he looked to see if I was kidding. When he saw I wasn't, he said solemnly, "No, Misha, Zina and I are not going together."

"How about Wilder?"

"Wilder! No, no, no! You dear, dear boy, you've fallen in love. You're blushing like a virgin."

"I'm *not* a virgin."

"I said *like*. Oh, dear lord!"

"You swear you're not going with her."

"I swear it, you poor creature. Nor is Wilder. Wouldn't he be amused! When did this dreadful thing happen? You can tell Henry. Henry is a friend of love. You can tell Henry absolutely everything."

I did, practically. He listened closely, clicking his tongue in disapproval at points, like Zina removing the leaf and encouraging me to sleep with Melissa. "How do you feel about sleeping with Melissa?"

"I did."

"And?"

"I didn't want to."

"You want to sleep with Zina."

"No!"

"Yes! Listen to me, Misha. You still think there's something sinful about love. And in fact there is, if you feel there is. Also, you think Zina has already slept with men, and you don't want to be like the others. You're different, your love is different. . . ."

"Has she slept with men?"

"If she hasn't she has a problem. So let's say for her own good she has."

"I just want to know if she's in love with someone now."

"Why do you think she might be?"

I told him what she said about being in peril and losing control and wanting me to protect her.

"That's rather sophisticated of you to conclude she's in love."

"Will you find out for me?"

"You mean if and who?"

"You don't know already, you swear it."

"I swear it. But tell me something first. Why would knowing help?"

"If she isn't in love it would be better, is all."

"And if she is?"

"If she is, she is."

"About the who. You wouldn't shoot him, would you? Or her?"

"Shoot Zina?"

"I didn't quite mean that. I meant if the him turned out to be a her. But I mustn't joke. All right, I'll try, and I'll tell you if I honorably can."

"How do you mean?"

"I can't very well tell you something told to me in confidence. Misha, how old are you?"

"Sixteen."

"You're certainly old enough for love, but you must know

somewhere deep down that this is not likely to work out."

"I don't care."

"Of course you care. But you have no choice."

"No, I have no choice."

"All right, I'll try to find out, not to satisfy your curiosity, but because it's better to know. And I have another reason. It's this. I don't think your personality is fully formed. You're an extremely intelligent and very attractive young man and grown up in many ways, but in other ways you're not grown up. Your destiny has not been decided. Do you know what I'm talking about?"

I said yes, but I didn't.

"In a word, your hash has not been settled, and this may settle it. We'll go to my place, and we'll find out, for better or worse. Okay?"

Like Father and me, Henry was a water person. Besides having the Chelsea Hotel, he lived in a houseboat moored not far from the restaurant. It was mostly one room, with a lot of portholes. You could feel the boat shifting and hear the slap of the water against the hull.

"The only problem with it," Henry said, "is rats occasionally come aboard, including the two-legged kind."

He pointed me into a sling chair, gave me a glass of vodka, and dialed Zina at the Point. "I have to get her talking without actually asking questions."

He held up his hand. "Darling, you know I'm psychic. . . . Yes, psycho too. You remember that dream I had, you were a siren singing at passing ships, and the next evening three Greek sailors came on to you. I was absolutely prescient. . . . Yes, precious too. Listen, darling, last night I dreamt you came to me wrapped in a sheet. . . . A bed sheet. Or maybe it was a winding sheet, and you said you were in trouble. . . . You didn't say. . . . What you said was you were losing control. . . ."

I waved my hands and shook my head. He was using the same words. She would know.

He patted the air reassuringly. "I *knew* it. Tell Henry everything."

So she *was* in love. He listened, grunting every now and then. What was ominous, he only looked at me twice during the whole thing, and then quickly looked away. He said nothing, except for things like, "Say that part again" and "I don't think so." Finally his voice rose to close the conversation, "All right, sweetie. . . . Yes, of course. . . . We'll talk," and he hung up.

"Well, you heard it," he said.

"Who is it?"

"She didn't say who."

"She talked and talked and didn't say who?"

He held his palms up hopelessly.

133

"You *know*."

"Misha, please."

"Why don't you tell me?"

I think I was shouting, and I think he was a little frightened.

"Misha, I have lots to say to you, but you're in no condition to listen. I want to help you, and I can, but you've got to quiet down. Why don't you absorb the basic fact, and then we can talk."

"You *know*."

"Misha, go home!"

13

Hillyer's Theory

I WENT TO Hillyer's place and told him the whole thing. I wanted to hear him talk about how love didn't exist. Instead he talked about who Zina was in love with.

"How do you know she really told this guy? He says she didn't."

"I heard everything he said. He didn't once ask her. He would have asked her."

"So why do you want to know?"

"Henry asked that. Look, if it's an old boyfriend, say, it wouldn't be so bad."

"Bad as what?"

"Somebody new."

"How do you figure that?"

"Or suppose it's this guy Henry himself. That wouldn't be serious either. He knows about art and photography. It could be they just have things in common."

"Why would he go through all this calling up and every-thing?"

"To lead me off the track. He's a good-looking guy. It could be him."

"All right, phone him. I'll get on the extension. Tell him how bad you feel. Sound suicidal. Tell him you'd feel better if you knew, no matter who it was. Tell him you never felt so bad."

"I never have."

"Good, you'll sound convincing."

Henry was back at his gallery. I pleaded with him.

"Misha, you're breaking my heart. Put it in the freezer. A few weeks from now, when you look there, it will be gone. I know you feel bad, but it won't last, I promise you. I've had plenty of experience in this department. Listen, Misha, tonight you come to the boat, and I'll cook dinner, and we'll talk. I have a lot of things I want to say to you."

"Will you tell me?"

"We'll talk."

"But will you tell me?"

"Tonight, seven o'clock. We'll open a wine from heaven."

I said I'd let him know and hung up.

"It's him," I said, "I know it."

"It's not him, he's a queer."

"How do you know that?"

"That's a homo voice if I ever heard one."

I didn't entirely know what homosexuals did.

"Also he's after your ass. He'll cook dinner, a wine from heaven, with music by candlelight. Come *on!*" Hillyer stood up and started pacing around the living room. "Let's work this through. First he agrees to find out. You even said he was eager. And he finds out. . . ."

"We don't absolutely know that."

"Yes, we do. You were sure when you came here, and I'm sure now. On the phone now, he didn't deny it."

"Maybe he's a homosexual," I said, "and she loves him anyhow."

"No, she's known him too long. Why now? Maybe if they fell into bed together. But he's queer. That wouldn't happen." He began picking his nose, a sign of concentration in Hillyer.

"If you weren't here," he said, "and I learned about this from someone else, you would be a prime suspect."

"Is that a joke?"

"Look at the evidence. You were on the spot, you liked her, she liked you. . . . Holy Christ, you know who it is? It's your old man. In situ."

My body went cold. "Impossible."

"Possible," he said.

"When could they have done it?"

"What do you mean, when could they have done it? How long does it take?"

"I don't mean *it*. I mean when could they have fallen in love?"

"You're the one who knows about love," Hillyer said, "you tell me."

"It's not possible."

"It's the one and only reason this guy won't tell you."

"It doesn't mean they actually *did* anything."

"Oh, no? The other night, when you went to her place, she wasn't there, right? And your old man was here in town, right? When you were screwing Melissa he was screwing Zina. Fair is fair."

Was it possible I was being punished for having slept with Melissa?

"Your father is obviously one of the great swordsmen."

This seemed to make Father even more of a hero to Hillyer.

"I have to think about this," I said.

"Think away. But if you faced the fact that love is an illusion you wouldn't mind so much. You might even get a kick out of it."

"You sure get a kick out of it."

"Hey, you enjoyed yourself, why shouldn't he?"

"I didn't enjoy myself."

I didn't know why I was even talking with Hillyer. "I'm going home."

"How do you feel?"

"Not so good." I stood up. It was hard to move.

"Stick around. Rita's coming over, we'll get Melissa."

"I don't think so. I'm going home."

"Are you okay?"

"I'm okay."

The apartment felt especially empty. I went upstairs to my parents' bedroom. On Mother's bureau was the picture of Father when he graduated from college. He was standing on the campus lawn shading his eyes. He didn't look much different from now. I don't think Mother had met him yet. On Father's bureau was the picture of me the day we caught the fluke. I was nine that summer; it was early July. Mr. Strangfeld said the fluke were running. Fluke are bottom fish, so we took the rowboat. Father said he had never seen anything like it. We dropped a line and pulled up a fluke. We put on two hooks and pulled up two. When we ran out of clams we cut up the fluke for bait. Father said fish don't ordinarily bite on their own meat, but they did then. We kept a fungo bat in the boat to put fish out of their misery when we hauled them aboard. Father usually did the whacking. But that day I did it. I'd whack one and he'd cheer. We beached the boat and took the fluke back in the wagon from the boathouse. It was so full they kept slipping off onto the sand. At the house Father took the picture of me with the fluke. There are a lot of pictures of me from that time. In this one I look really happy.

Standing in the bedroom, I wanted to do two opposite things: figure this out and not think about it. I don't know how long I stood there, but when I began to imagine Father and Zina in this bed together I called Henry and said I would like to come for dinner.

When I got there, Henry was in an apron at the stove. He pointed to the sling chair. "Vodka?"

"I don't really like drinking that much, Henry. Maybe just the wine with dinner." If Hillyer was right this was the first homosexual I knew was a homosexual.

"Then we can really talk. Now let's just chat."

"Can I ask you something in the meantime?"

"Talk or chat?"

"When you were on the phone and Zina didn't tell who it was, why didn't you ask her?"

"Because, my dear Misha, because she said specifically, 'I can't tell you who it is.' That's why. You remind me of a friend of mine. The same problem, except that he's twice your age. Six months ago he sat exactly where you're sitting and he told me he couldn't go on, it was all over, he didn't want to live."

"Did the girl fall in love with someone else?"

"He was devastated. And today there are no scars, he has another companion, and he can hardly remember the first one's name. The special point I want to make is that you are half his age and will heal twice as fast. You don't think so now, but there won't be a mark on you, you'll be as beautiful as ever." He said all this with his back to me.

"A friend of mine thinks Zina is in love with my father."

He spun around. "What a *grotesque* idea!"

"Then it isn't my father."

"Misha, it could be the man in the moon for all I know. Let's eat."

He lit candles, as Hillyer said he would, and turned on music. He asked me what I thought of the wine.

"Chateauneuf du Pape," I said.

"Very *good*."

"Nineteen-fifty-eight."

"Oh, you naughty boy, you looked." He touched the back of my hand. "Misha dear, let me tell you something. In stories there's a magic potion that puts you to sleep. When you wake up you fall in love with the first person you see. That is the most brilliant metaphor of love there is. Love is arbitrary, inexplicable, and cruel. It is also impermanent. Nothing so unreasonable could possibly last long."

"It's not unreasonable that I'm in love with Zina. She is the most beautiful girl I've ever seen."

"Exactly my point. She is the most beautiful girl you've ever seen because you fell in love with her."

"She was beautiful before."

"And, pray, when did you fall in love?"

"As soon as I saw her."

"Voilà! Misha, there's nothing wrong with hurting for a little while. Everyone has their heart broken. For some people it's a way of life. Love feels like a ray that goes from you to someone else. Sometimes it's returned, and sometimes not. But love is not a ray. It's a burst of light that goes out in all directions. It seems to shine on one object because the lover sees only one object. But if the lover looks around he'll see that many objects catch his light." He touched my hand again.

I had to get out of there.

Before he served the coffee I said I didn't feel well and I had to get back to my dog. He said I should lie down until I felt better. I got out finally by promising to come back soon.

Then on the way home I figured the whole thing out. It was completely my idea that Zina was in love with someone.

Henry went along with it and faked the call to Zina so he could come on to me. He hadn't spoken to her at all, and now he wouldn't tell me who it was because there was no one. She wasn't in love with anyone.

14

What Zina Said

THE IDEA DIDN'T last.

From the apartment I called the Point to say I was staying in town overnight. I got into bed to think. The morning Father had been short with me he said that when I was coming to town I must always tell him. Did he mean *warn* him? He hadn't been concerned the night he took a woman into the guestroom, but he sure would care if I knew about Zina. This was real evidence.

Finally I realized I wasn't going to figure it out. But maybe I could figure out an attitude that would help me feel better. For instance, what attitude should I have if it really was Father? Or if Zina just had a crush on him that he didn't know about. Things like this went around in my head until I remembered Mrs. Mertz's advice: Ask her, she'll tell you.

So at 1 A.M. I got dressed and went down to the marina. The Angela was motionless in the still water. "Dover Beach" came back to me as I ran up the sails.

> The sea is calm tonight.
> The tide is full, the moon lies fair
> Upon the straits. . . .

The bay was calm, the tide was out, the sails hung slack. I drifted into the bay. Without a wind I'd eventually be carried out to sea, where a sudden change of weather could be dangerous for a one-man crew. I didn't care. I was going to find out, one way or another. Then a breeze came up. There was no moonlight or starlight. I tacked across the bay using the one light on the Point, probably from Mr. Strangfeld's shack. Walking over the sand, I felt a little better. Nothing was certain yet.

Both houses were dark. I took off my shoes and left them on the porch. Blackheart heard me. I let him out and told him to be quiet. On the way to the guesthouse everything had a silvery tinge, but not enough to see shapes by. Across the bay a faint line of light stretched over the mainland. Otherwise I might have had my eyes shut. I made out Sonya asleep on the deck. Blackheart settled down in front of her, nose to nose.

I held the catch on the screen door and let myself in. There were two bedrooms. I didn't know which was Zina's and which was Mrs. Mertz's. I inched along in the dark and made my way into the near one. I stood in what I guessed was the center of the room, perfectly still, perfectly quiet. My plan had been to gently say her name until she woke. In that way I wouldn't frighten her. Now the plan changed. If she was here in bed I would slide in beside her the way Melissa had beside me. She would turn to me as I had to Melissa. At first she wouldn't know who I was. Somebody from the past maybe, like the boy with the Chinese eyes. She would put her arms around me. "It's me," I'd say. "Oh, Misha, what are you doing here? You're in my bed. You naughty boy." No, she wouldn't say that. She'd kiss me. She had kissed me often. She'd kiss me now. She would have nothing on. I'd run my hand down her back. Her breasts would be pressed against my chest. I'd pull her away and touch them. She'd say my name, once and then again and again.

I was very excited. If the plan worked, we could meet at her place in town in the winter or at my place when my parents were away. It would be our secret. Maybe I'd let Hillyer in on it. I'd tell her how I had suspected Father and Henry. She'd stroke my face and say, "Poor Misha, it was you all along."

I could see nothing but the outline of the window. I felt a chair, a chest of drawers, and then my knees touched the bed. I listened for breathing. My ears were full of my own breathing. I knelt down and put my hand on the coverlet. The bed was flat and empty. She was in the other bedroom.

I stood up. The plan hung on her being asleep. Otherwise I wouldn't have the nerve to go through with it. I turned around and took slow, small, careful steps toward the doorway.

In the other room Zina said, "Peter, I'm in here," and after a pause, "In here, Peter."

At that moment a light went on in the main house. I thought of Melissa's poem, "a light makes darkness clearly black."

I stood still. I don't think I could have moved even if I knew what to do. I waited for something else to happen. Would Father show up? Would she say it again, "Peter, I'm in here"? Would he get into bed with her? Would she turn to him and pull him on top of her? Would I have to hear the sounds?

I rushed out. I didn't care if she knew it was me or not. On the deck Blackheart jumped up and followed me to the house. Mother was sitting at the kitchen table with a book and a cup of tea. I called through the screen to say I was home.

I explained that I couldn't sleep in town. She poured tea for me and said she couldn't sleep either. I asked where Father was.

"Upstairs, probably tossing and turning like the rest of us. Usually he walks on the beach when he can't sleep, whereas I come down here and get fat. It's not fair."

Looking at her, puffy and huddled in a pink wrapper, I saw for the first time how unfair it was. She was having a rotten life, always jealous, not knowing what was going on, but knowing something was. And him up there, disappointed this time but planning the next time.

"I was thinking about us," Mother said, "you and your father and me. I suppose it's these feelings you have for Zina that set me thinking. There'll be Zina Two and Zina Three, and all of a sudden you'll be gone. I don't know if you know it, but you're the main attraction for your father in this house. The reason he and I were awake tonight was that you weren't here. I worry when you're alone in town, but your father just plain misses you. I should go upstairs and tell him you're back."

"No, don't. He's probably asleep by now."

"You know, two people get together and have a kid. There's never enough time, never enough sleep. Somehow you get through it. Then things get easier. What was impossible becomes possible. You can see a year ahead. At the start you couldn't see to the weekend. Now you know what's coming, all too well."

"Are you and Father having trouble?"

"Oh, baby, these are night thoughts, not stuff to lay on my kid."

"If something happened, would you marry someone else?"

"An heir to millions. Now look, you don't have to sit around here keeping me company. Go to bed."

But I did have to. I got a book, and we both stayed up till dawn.

Next day when I came downstairs, in the early afternoon, Mother was spread out on the oceanside porch. She said Father was at the bay. Then through the kitchen window I saw Zina walking in that direction. I let Blackheart come along, and we followed her. I was careful to keep dunes between us so if she turned around I could drop down. From behind the boathouse I watched her stand at the foot of the dock. Father in the water beside the Angela watched her too. After a while she walked out, stopping once as if to go back. He helped her into the water. I waited for a sign of intimacy, a kiss, a touch. But they stood apart, facing each other. Nothing else was in sight, no people, no boats moving in the bay. The sky was gray, and the seaweed gave off its damp, rotting smell.

Suddenly he slapped her. She put her hand to her cheek and examined it as if looking for blood. Then the most remarkable thing—she kissed the palm of her hand. He turned away from her, and she waded toward shore. Blackheart raced past me and out onto the dock. Bending low and keeping the boathouse behind me, I hurried back to the house. In a little while Father showed up. He looked at me severely and said nothing. This was not the person I knew. Whatever else he did, my father didn't hit people.

15

The Labor Day Party

THE LABOR DAY party was two days later.

One of its traditions was Father's ferry service to and from town. This year we picked up Hillyer and Mr. Walton. We brought the Angela into the marina about noon. It was a brilliantly blue, gusty day. Mr. Walton was dressed for the occasion in Bermuda shorts, Topsiders, a nautical cap. He carried a small duffel bag printed with anchors. As usual, he apologized for his wife, the beautiful Elaine, who couldn't make it.

In the open water Father asked him to bless the boat. Mr. Walton leaned over the gunnels to see the Angela's name. "Dear Lord," he said, "keep this proud boat, the Angela, shipshape, seaworthy, and snug. As she mounts the waves and embraces the wind, may she always ride high, reach port, and be ever eager to take to the sea once more." We applauded.

A strong gust suddenly tipped the Angela far over. Mr. Walton gripped the rail with both hands.

"Don't worry, padre," Father said, "the Lord provides."

Mr. Walton held on tight and said, " 'And when Peter was come down out of the ship, he walked on the water, to go to Jesus. But when he saw the wind boisterous, he was afraid; and beginning to sink, he cried, saying, "Lord, save me." And immediately Jesus stretched forth his hand, and caught him, and said unto him, "O thou of little faith, wherefore didst thou doubt?" ' "

"For faith shall make thee buoyant, is that the way it works, padre?"

"Yes indeed." But he continued to hang on.

Father seemed strained and his good humor forced. As we approached the Point he asked Hillyer if he had changed his mind about love.

"Not yet, sir, but I could see how I might."

"You've met Miss Right?"

"Yes, sir, in a way."

"I trust she's a virgin."

"Hard to say, sir. I was thinking of Zina."

I couldn't believe Hillyer's nerve.

Father looked quickly at me and then at Hillyer. "You think you could care for Zina," he said.

"That's about it, sir."

"You find her attractive."

"Powerfully attractive. But what would you say about the virgin aspect, sir?"

"Your guess is as good as mine, Hillyer."

"No, sir, your guess would be better."

"Why so?"

"My experience is with younger females, as you know, sir."

"Well, Hillyer, I wouldn't want to venture an opinion."

"Is that because you don't have one, sir, or because of neighborly reticence?"

This really got to Father. He knew he was being baited, and he thought I was in on it. I wasn't. Nor had I told Hillyer about the guesthouse or anything else that had happened.

As we pulled up to the dock the Cuddihys were landing a dinghy from their boat. Melissa fell in beside me as we walked across the Point. She said Ari had asked her to go steady, did I mind? I said Ari was a very nice guy. And a good poet, she added. He had written her a beautiful poem, did I want to see it? I said it might be difficult for me to read it. I couldn't have cared less about Melissa and Ari, but out of politeness I tried to look glum.

Mr. Strangfeld had picked up the two other Point couples, the Kanes and the Rugers, and delivered them to the party. The Chelsea Hotel had arrived and was anchored in the ocean beyond the waves. Henry, Wilder, Jack Packard, and Max Pondoro—Mrs. Mertz's crowd—and Mrs. Mertz herself were on the ocean porch with Mother; they had just swum in from the boat. There was also a young friend of Henry's named Sandro. He was very good-looking, but there was something wrong with him. He had no expression, and he struck poses one after the other. Listening he turned his profile, talking he looked you full in the face. No one else seemed to notice this but Father, who saw me watching and gave me his big smile. We had been staying out of one another's way. This was like old times.

Mother had asked Zina to take pictures, and now she moved from person to person and group to group. Mr. Strangfeld was always exuberant at the Labor Day parties. He was a big, barrel-chested man, and this year he showed up in a T-shirt that read "Dollar a Kiss." Sandro went up to him, kissed him on the lips, and pranced away. Mr. Strangfeld wiped his mouth and clenched his fists. I thought he would go after Sandro. Mother must have thought so too, because she rushed up to Mr. Strangfeld and kissed him. This undid Sandro's kiss, and he relaxed. Zina caught the whole thing. She then approached Father with camera raised. He turned away. She followed him. He turned away. She looked like she had been slapped again.

Another tradition of the Labor Day party was getting lunch from the bay. The year before, it was mussels. We filled four pails, more than we could eat. Mrs. Yemm got a bad one and was sick. Mother said she deserved it for trying to muscle in on her marriage. Some years we dug for piss clams. Small holes showed up here and there in the wet sand at low tide. When you stepped next to one a stream of water shot up your leg and you knew a steamer was underneath. We served piss clams with melted butter and clam broth. They were the best dish. Then there were spearing, bait fish that swam in schools and tended to stay near shore away from the big fish. We caught them in a dragnet and fried them in boiling oil. I liked them plain, but some people were squeamish about eating the eyes, so before cooking them we rolled them in flour and ate them like pretzel sticks.

Now, as if to get away from Zina, Father asked Hillyer to go with him for spearing. I usually went. It was almost a ritual. Father was getting away from me too.

As soon as Father left, Zina came up to me. She wanted to take a picture, she said, and suggested we go to the bay porch, where the light was better.

She looked agitated. "Misha, I must ask you for something. But you mustn't be cruel to me."

"I'm never cruel to you."

"You mustn't be now." She put her palms together. "You were in the guesthouse Friday night. I saw you from my window when you left. I said something. What was it?"

"You know what you said."

"I was half asleep."

"You were wide awake."

"Misha, tell me, please!"

"You said, 'I'm in here, Peter.' "

"What did that mean?"

"Why are you doing this?"

"Tell me what it meant!"

"You thought it was Father. You were waiting for my father."

"Keep your voice down! Misha, I'm going to tell you something very terrible. I'm in love with your father."

"I know that. Were you going to sleep with him?"

"We just wanted to be together."

"In your bedroom? In the middle of the night?"

"I don't know what we were going to do."

"Should we ask *him*? Let's ask him."

"You're being cruel, Misha."

"You're not being fair. You're asking me things, but you won't tell me anything. Have you slept with him? Tell me that!"

"That doesn't matter when you love someone."

"It matters to me. I'm sure it matters to him."

"Misha, you say you love me."

"I don't say that. I *loved* you."

"All right, loved me. But you know how it feels. I love your father."

"You said that. Why are we doing this? What do you want?"

"I want you to help me. Your father thinks you know about us."

"I didn't tell him."

"I told him. I made the terrible mistake of telling him what I said in the guesthouse and that you probably know."

"What did he say?"

"He was furious. He said, 'How could you be so stupid?'"

"And he hit you."

"You saw that? Yes, he hit me, and now he won't speak to me. Will you help me?"

"Doing what?"

"I want you to make him think you don't know."

"You want me to say, 'Father, I don't know you're sleeping with Zina'?"

"No. Listen! He's not sure, and if you ask him, very seriously, very carefully, *Are you having an affair with Zina's mother?*, he'll think you don't know."

"So you can sleep with him again."

Her face, which was always serene, was pinched now, as if in shame. "You could blackmail me. Is that what you want?"

"What do you mean?"

"You could make me sleep with you. Is that what you want?"

"That's not what I want. I wanted *you*."

She studied me for a few seconds, then said, "You know, Misha, you're half woman. . . . I mean that as a compliment." She stepped close to embrace me. "You'll do it? For me?"

I turned out of her arms and went back to the party.

She joined her mother and Henry. In a minute Henry came over to me, took me by the elbow, and led me onto the sand. "Misha dear, I apologize. I lied because I wanted to protect you."

"It's all right. I don't love her anymore."

"Are you sure?"

"I'm sure."

"My advice is find someone as unlike Zina as possible, and do it immediately."

"All right, Henry, thanks."

I climbed back onto the porch. It wasn't over. Mrs. Mertz took me aside. She removed her sunglasses. "Can you take some advice from an old crone?"

I nodded.

"Now that you know what's up, you must keep control of yourself. Do you understand what I'm saying?"

I nodded.

"If you don't, everyone will lose, including you."

"I've already lost."

"You can't lose what you never had. But you can lose your father, and he can lose you."

"Hasn't that happened?"

"Does your mother know anything about this?"

"She thinks you're the dangerous woman."

"I'm flattered. Let me tell you about dangerous women. Let's say your father and I had it off and got caught. Your mother might sit for it. But if he gets caught with a twenty-year-old girl, she will not sit for it. Your mother and I are at a tender age. We're still in business, but we don't know for how long. A middle-aged woman competing with a middle-aged woman is quite different from competing with a girl. Do you want your parents to stay together?"

"Yes."

"Then you must master your feelings. Can you do that?"

"I don't know."

"Do you want to try?"

"I don't know that either."

"Well, you can only do what you can do, and you can only do what you want to do."

"Okay, I'll try," I said.

Father and Hillyer were back with the spearing, which Mother and one of her helpers were preparing in the kitchen. Suddenly from nowhere Blackheart rushed to Sonya, who had been sitting upright on the porch in the midst of the guests. In a kind of consent she lowered her belly to the floor. He covered her behind. It couldn't have been the real thing because her tail was down. Mr. Strangfeld called out, *"Gut gemacht, Schwarzherz!"* Everyone was transfixed by Blackheart's enterprise. When he finally backed off, there were theatrical sighs and cheers. Zina, who stood in front of me and behind Father, touched his hand. He drew it away.

There were lots of other things to eat besides spearing. Lunch went on all afternoon because there wouldn't be any supper. Mother always made it clear that these were Labor *Day* parties. The drinkers started on the wine and liquor. Some of those in bathing suits went swimming in the ocean. Although the sky was still clear and the air warm, a wind off the ocean picked up to a steady fifteen knots. As I stood talking to Mother, I saw Zina was waiting to get me alone again.

"I have something else to say to you, Misha. You understand that the reason your father is upset is that he loves you and doesn't want to see you hurt."

"Sometimes he looks like he hates me."

"He *loves* you, Misha. What you see in his face are your own feelings. If you do this for me, if you convince him you don't know, you'll be helping him, don't you see?"

"Why should I help him? Why shouldn't I help myself? Did you mean it about sleeping with me?"

She said nothing.

"Yes or no?"

"That wasn't an offer, Misha."

"I want to blackmail you. Did you mean it or not?"

"Yes."

"All right, let's do it."

"Before you do your part?"

"Yes."

"You don't trust me. You want payment first."

"Will you do it?"

"Where?"

"Upstairs. Now."

"Misha, this is not like you. We can't do it upstairs."

"In the boat then."

"Wait till tonight."

"No. In the boat. Now."

"You're angry."

"I'm not angry. And I'm not half woman. Will you do it, yes or no?"

She waited so long, I thought she would say no. But she

said, "Give me five minutes." She went to the guesthouse.

After two or three minutes Hillyer came up to me and said, "They're gone."

"Who?"

"Your old man and Zina."

"I don't think so."

"What do you mean, you don't think so? Everyone else is here."

I took him to the kitchen door. There was Father talking to Mother.

"Okay, but where is she?"

"Hillyer, go eat something."

I didn't see Zina go to the boat, but the five minutes were up. Mother called from the kitchen, "Michael, will you help with the drinks?"

"In a little while, Mother?"

"No fuss, your father will do it."

As I stepped onto the sand Blackheart came rushing around from the ocean side. Wherever I was going he was going.

The Angela was tipping from side to side. I told Blackheart to stay. He knew when there was no appeal and sat down on the dock, excited, his tail twitching. He seemed to be saying to me, "Now you!" I was ashamed of the thought. I wanted to sleep with Zina, but also the idea occurred to me that maybe I would be undoing what Father had done, the way Mother had undone Sandro's kiss.

I opened the cabin door. Zina was lying naked, face up, pressed to one side of the bunk. Her eyes were closed and her hands crossed on her chest like a corpse. I stood there, waiting for her to look at me and say something. But she didn't move. I got out of my bathing suit and lay down beside her. I put my hand on her. She pushed it away and said, "Let's just do it." Her voice was cold and flat. I didn't care. I raised myself on my hands to get on top of her, but she arranged it so that we did it on our side. She kept her eyes closed all through it. Before it was over I knew I had made a terrible mistake, but the sweetness of it filled me, excluding everything else.

Afterwards I waited for her to say something, if only my name. But she didn't. I wanted to tell her I loved her. But instead I said I was sorry. She didn't even say it was all right. What she said finally was, "You'll do it now, won't you?" I said I would.

A volleyball game started on the beach. Zina joined Mr. Strangfeld's team. The only sign that we had been together was a quick, pleading look she gave me. Mrs. Mertz caught my eye and gave me a thumbs-up signal, as if to strengthen my resolve to master my feelings. Hillyer nodded to me knowingly, like one spy to another. He was still looking for clues.

Whatever Zina had felt for me I had destroyed. I walked into the ocean and pulled my trunks away from my body so that the salt water would circulate and wash away the mistake.

At five o'clock heavy clouds blew in from the north. Some people were still swimming. Father waved them out, and when lightning and rain came we all took cover on the porch. I wanted this party to be done and the summer to be done.

16

Getting Over Things

BY SEVEN THE rain had stopped and the party was ending. The Chelsea Hotel had taken off with its passengers. Mr. Strangfeld had returned the Kanes and the Rugers to their houses. Hillyer and the Cuddihys were staying the night. Mr. Walton pulled on a pair of slacks for the trip to town. Melissa and Ari went with us. The air was cool now, the wind still brisk. Father managed the sails, and I took the tiller. Mr. Walton asked if anyone knew a sea chanty. Father suggested "Row, Row, Row Your Boat." At the marina, as Ari helped Melissa onto the dock, she gave me the saddest look. Or maybe it was the fading light.

Father had been avoiding me. Now, sailing back to the

Point, he talked, but offhandedly. How had my summer been? How did I think it had gone for Mother? Should we invite the Mertzes back next year? Was I looking forward to school? Did I know who my teachers would be? Is Hillyer really such a devil with the ladies? This was unlike him. Father didn't go in for small talk, or even plain talk; everything he said had a twist. He could see I was uneasy. I was making perfunctory responses and watching him closely. He was watching me even more closely. This too was unlike him. Father took things in glancingly. As it was, he looked in the moonlight like an eager ghost.

I decided to get my part of the bargain over with. I asked him Zina's question.

We had swung out into the ocean and now were sailing southeast toward the Rocks on the bayside. The wind was whipping along, and the water was noisy. He asked me to repeat what I had said.

"That's some question, Michael. It might have been more appropriate from another member of the family, wouldn't you say? I thought we agreed that a gentleman never tells."

He had turned playful, but he meant to leave the impression that the answer to my question was yes.

"Michael, you have your own ideas on the subject. You should know mine. I'm not Don Giovanni, women are not food and drink to me. But they do do something important.

They mark the passing years. They are like writing for a writer, winning elections for a politician. They make time memorable, they keep it from dissolving into nothing. Do you understand what I'm saying?"

"I understand the words. But you're talking about sex, not love."

"There's no real distinction. A 'heightened' experience tends to be love, a lesser one sex."

"On a scale of one to ten."

"We're talking about feelings, Michael, not weight lifting. Something happened last spring at a lawn party in town. It was a perfect Sunday afternoon, warm in the sun, cool in the shade. Everyone had a glass in their hand. A man came up to the woman next to me and said, 'I *know* you.' 'I was your second wife,' she said."

"Were they drunk?"

"The point I'm making is that sometimes profound experiences end in indifference."

"Are you talking about Mrs. Mertz or what?"

"I'm talking about life, Michael. I'm talking about myself and you and everyone."

"About Zina and me?"

"In a way."

"Everybody's been telling me how people get over things. Maybe you can get over this. I slept with Zina in this boat this afternoon. There's a stain on the bunk to prove it. Go look!"

Father lashed the mainsheet to a cleat on the gunnel so the boat would hold by itself. He stood up. At first I thought he was actually going to look. Then I thought he wanted to hurt me. He seemed immense. I yanked the tiller. The boom swung across the deck, slowly at first and then fast. He tried to duck, but it hit him in the head, and he went over backwards and disappeared. The Angela swerved sharply toward the Rocks. I lost control and almost capsized. By dropping the tiller and catching the butt of the boom I turned the Angela into the wind and steadied her. I had to get back to where he went over. I did a figure eight, tacking southeast and northwest. On the last tack I slammed into the Rocks and tore a hole in the Angela's port side. Water flooded in, and she sank to the gunnels. Whitecaps in the moonlight looked like Father and then didn't. Being wood, the boat didn't go under but lumbered in the tide away from the Rocks. I stepped, more than dove, into the water. The Rocks were as slippery as fish. To make it harder I was climbing Three Rock Edge. I lost my hold, hit my forehead, scraped my legs, and was back in the water. By swimming north I managed to clamber up. The Angela looked like a broken toy, tipping sluggishly and moving half sunk out to sea.

I saw nothing on the surface but the whitecaps. I waited

until there was no chance. I took off my deck shoes and started back toward the beach. Three Rock Edge was right in front of me, and, like the first time, I sat down and inched across. It wasn't that I was frightened, I had to make sure I got home to call the Coast Guard. Waves sent up spray from the oceanside. I suppose I was crying. Tears and salt water taste the same.

I ran all the way to the house. As I opened the screen door, there were Mother, Zina, Mrs. Mertz, the Cuddihys, and Hillyer. I saw in their faces what they saw in mine. Something bad had happened.

Mr. Cuddihy called the Coast Guard and put me on. Everyone gathered around to hear the details. Mother wiped my bloody forehead with a wet towel. When I told how the boom had swung across the deck I looked up at Zina. The others were just listening. But I could see into Zina's eyes, and she into mine, and she knew.

When I told the Coast Guard all I could I looked for her. No one had seen her go. I was sure she had gone to the Rocks to look for Father.

"She'll kill herself," Mr. Cuddihy said.

He and Hillyer and I hurried down to the beach. She was not in sight.

"How do you know she went to the Rocks?" Mr. Cuddihy said.

"I know," I said.

"I know too," Hillyer said, and the three of us ran as fast as we could. I should have been out of breath, but I didn't even feel my body.

At the Rocks I told the others to wait. Mr. Cuddihy protested, but Hillyer said they'd only complicate things. Once on the Rocks I could see her, half way out, picking her way with her arms extended for balance. The stone was very slippery from the earlier rain. I tested my footing at every step. When I reached her I took her hand. She turned around with no resistance, and I guided her back. Walking along the beach, none of us spoke. There was nothing to say.

Mrs. Mertz took Zina to the guesthouse. Mrs. Cuddihy put a bandage on my head and cleaned the blood off my legs. Mother was on the phone with the Coast Guard. They said they would keep the line open from the search boat for as long as she wanted. We all stayed up, and at dawn Hillyer, Mr. Cuddihy, and I walked the bay and ocean beaches till noon.

Everyone agreed we should go back to town. I heard Mr. Cuddihy say to Hillyer that Mother shouldn't be around in case the body washed up. That afternoon Mr. Strangfeld took the Mertzes to the train and then us to our car.

17

Conclusions

THE LOCAL WEEKLY came out on Thursday. Father was the main story. It didn't say that he was dead, only that the Coast Guard had given up the search, which amounted to the same thing. Father's biography was a kind of obituary. Forty-four, born in 1919, in Neptune, New Jersey, graduated from Rutgers. Nothing I didn't know, except Neptune was a strange coincidence.

Father wasn't found, so we didn't have a regular funeral. A month later Mr. Walton phoned to say he would be speaking about Father the following Sunday, perhaps we'd like to come and invite our friends. Mrs. Cuddihy was staying with Mother and did the inviting. Word got around, and the

Church of the Fishers of Men filled up.

Mr. Walton really liked Father, and his comments were warm and sincere. He said how charming, loved, admired, respected, et cetera, Father was, and he wanted to tell a little story that also showed how generous he was. It seems that a few years back Mrs. Walton, the beautiful Elaine, was planning to go to business school and start a second career, and Father invited her to his office twice a week so she could see how business was really conducted. At the mention of Mrs. Walton, Mother tightened up beside me, and after the service when she came up to offer condolences Mother went thin-lipped. I knew then why Mrs. Walton hadn't accompanied her husband to the Labor Day parties.

Mrs. Yemm got the same treatment. But Mrs. Mertz was okay. Mother stayed dry eyed until Zina approached. Then something loosened in her. They put their arms around one another and both broke down. Mother had no idea about Father and Zina, and she liked Zina and recognized certain things about herself in her.

I hadn't seen Zina since the night Father drowned. Now she touched my hand and said, "I'm sorry." So these were almost the last words we said to one another. But I really loved Zina, and you can't regret having loved someone.

Hillyer was there with some boys from school. He waved to me over the heads of people. He would have made a better son for Father. They could have matched wits and worked things out that way.

As I stood beside Mother and listened to expressions of sympathy, I sensed how unprotected we two were now. Father was the one who knew about the world, Mother and I didn't. Among all those friends, in that Christian church, we were alone.

As we walked home, she said she thought she hadn't been right for Father. He needed someone who was more fun. I said I thought she had been exactly right.

The Mertzes moved back to New York City. The others, as far as I know, are all alive except Mr. Cuddihy, Mr. Strangfeld, and Blackheart. Mother and I never used the house again, so we invited Mr. Strangfeld to live in it, which he did until he died, a few years ago. The government took over Bone Point on schedule and gave us some money for the house. The United States Weather Bureau uses it now. The other places were pulled down.

Over the years I've come to realize that I'm more like Mother than I ever was like Father. Mother, Melissa, and I were on the side of love where you could be hurt. Father, Mrs. Mertz, and Hillyer were on the other side. Zina probably thought she was on that side, but she wasn't.

I'm now older than Father was when he drowned. I don't know why I still feel like a child.